A Beautiful Place
for a Murder

Berlie Doherty

Five Leaves Publications
www.fiveleaves.co.uk

A Beautiful Place for a Murder
Berlie Doherty

Published in 2008
by Five Leaves Publications,
PO Box 8786, Nottingham NG1 9AW
info@fiveleaves.co.uk
www.fiveleaves.co.uk

ISBN: 978 1 905512 45 4

Five Leaves is a member of Inpress Books
(www.inpressbooks.co.uk),
representing independent publishers

Typeset by Four Sheets Design and Print
Printed in Great Britain

1

It was the first time my mum had left me on my own. Five days of glorious freedom stretched in front of me.

"Enjoy yourself," I shouted, waving her off. "Don't worry about me. I'll be fine!"

I danced back into the house, whooping with delight. And half an hour after she'd gone, I was plunged into the worst experience of my life.

She left just after breakfast. It was too early for my bus to school, which comes up to the farm near my house and picks up all the kids in the valley on its way back down. I decided not to wait for it, but to walk over to my girlfriend's house and catch it with her. Nobody knew she was my girlfriend, not even Caroline herself. This week would help to change all that. That was my plan. I would have loads of time to spend with her. Her mum and mine were close friends, and I'd known Caroline for years, even before we moved to Edale. And suddenly she was beautiful. How come I'd never noticed it before? How come her smile turned my bones to water?

So I set off with plenty of time to spare. The lane was still quiet. The early workers had gone into Sheffield or wherever, the hikers hadn't started flooding in. Apart from the drone of a tractor and the bleating of the sheep, the valley was silent. I love it like that. It was already hot, the September sky just about as blue as it could get. I gazed up at it, trying to remember whether Caroline's eyes were blue, and practising how I could tell her that they looked like the sky. Windows of the sky. Pools reflecting the sky.

It made me dizzy, so I looked down, and saw a green purse on the road, right at my feet. I glanced round quickly. Funny, how you get those prickly feelings, sure that someone's watching you. But there was no one in sight. I picked the purse up and opened it, feeling furtive and guilty as I did so. A quick look showed me that there was about a hundred pounds in notes, and quite a bulge of coins in the zip bit. No credit cards. A Derbyshire library card. I flipped it over. The signature was hard to read. Win Lingworth. The name sounded familiar, but I couldn't put a face to it. I had a feeling that was the name of the woman who lived in the little old house down by the railway cuttings — we called it the hidden cottage because it couldn't be seen from the road or the train, you had to know it was there.

I poked my fingers down inside another of the pockets. There was a 'cardiac alert' card, with an emergency number to call in case of a heart attack. That made me feel a bit strange, as if I knew a secret about somebody. A few receipts, two books of stamps. I looked round again, hoping that whoever had dropped it would come running back for it. Well, not running if they were about to suffer a heart attack. There was still no one, but still that strange sensation that I wasn't on my own.

I had several options now. I could keep the purse. Against my principles. I could keep some of the notes. Again, not my kind of thing. I could report the find to the police. That might mean having to trail into Sheffield or something. What a waste of a day. I could leave it where I'd found it. She might come back looking for it any minute. But someone else might find it who didn't have the same principles as me. Or I could return it myself.

If she did live in that hidden cottage it was hardly out of my way. I had to pass the track on my way to Caroline's, and I still had plenty of time to spare. It would be my good deed for the day. It would be something to tell Caroline about. It might impress her.

I set off at a jog and swung into the track that the hidden cottage shared with a farm. There were two wheelie bins and two mailboxes at the end of the track, where it met the lane. They were the only things that showed that anybody lived down there. After about a quarter of a mile the track split into two. One of them snaked off to the left, and the other, deeply rutted, swung to the right and plunged down into a shady hollow. I was confused; I'd never been down either way before, and I couldn't think which would be more likely. I decided to take the left-hand one, which looked better used. I came to a rickety five-bar gate with a broken hinge, and lifted it open carefully.

"Where d'you think you're going?" a man's voice bellowed across the field, and I retreated rapidly. A thickset, scowling farmer approached me. A dog with a hundred teeth loped, snarling, at his side.

"Sorry, I've come the wrong way," I shouted over my shoulder. What you learn round here is, some farmers are nice, some aren't, and they're all utterly charming when they think you're trespassing on their property.

I glanced at my watch. Still loads of time. I ran back to the other track, which soon plunged down into a hollow overhung with trees. The cottage was much further than I expected, if there was anything there at all, and I was just beginning to think that I'd gone completely wrong when I saw a woman's yellow cardigan or jacket of some sort lying in a big clump of nettles. It was humped over in a strange, bulky sort of way.

I felt a bit queasy, seeing that. There was no way I was going to put my hand in the clump for it, even if they hadn't been stinging nettles. What if someone was still wearing it? What if she'd realised that she'd lost her purse and had a cardiac arrest? I worked my way round the nettles and made quite sure it was just an empty jacket, then I found a branch lying on the ground and hooked the jacket up with it. It was quite light, with a weight of some sort in one of the pockets. I put my hand inside, and found a mobile phone.

If this belongs to Win Lingworth too, then she must be pretty careless, I thought, losing a purse and a jacket and a phone on the same day. It could hardly belong to anyone else. I couldn't imagine who might come up here, it was so overgrown. Well, I put the jacket over my arm and carried on up the track, and was very relieved when I saw the gate of the hidden cottage. Hooked over the post by a strand of orange twine was a pair of binoculars.

"She's mad," I thought. "She'd lose her head if it was loose, as Mum would say."

I left the binoculars where they were. She could find those for herself. The gate was standing open, but there were so many weeds pushing up round it that I doubt if it was ever closed. I went on up the twisty path to the front door. That was open too. Paint peeled away from the wood in dry flakes, like old skin.

I knocked loudly. "Miss Lingworth!" I shouted. "Miss Lingworth!"

The silence was like a waiting breath. I could hear my own heart beating into it. I went round to the back of the house. It was a jungle of weeds and flowers struggling together for light. There were the scorched remains of what must have been quite a large bonfire. A vegetable patch had almost gone to seed, but for a row of straggly potato plants. The leaves hung long and heavy, with a few seeded potatoes like little green Christmas baubles dangling on the ends of the trailing stalks. Butterflies danced everywhere as if it was their paradise. At the bottom of the garden was a large pond, the nearest edge strangely cleared of the dense jumble of weeds that clogged up the middle. A few lilies as white as little clouds sat on the dark water. And again, that deep, deep silence, except for the heavy droning and whining of insects.

I turned back towards the house and saw that the kitchen door was open. She must be there. I hammered on the door as loudly as I could, shouting her name, and when I stopped, the memory of my voice hung scared and strangled in the humming silence.

I stepped into the kitchen and put the jacket and the phone and purse on the table. I was surprised at how modern it looked inside, apart from an ancient black stove. It wasn't at all dingy and oldy-worldy like the outside. But that empty silence was unnerving. There was a strange, sharp rusty smell. Bluebottles buzzed round me as if the kitchen belonged to them. I turned and ran down the track, ran all the way to Caroline's, and just missed the bus.

Nothing is more annoying than missing the school bus. There's only one a day from here, taking all the older kids in the valley (about six of us) to Bakewell. Then it comes back and takes the younger kids to the local school. I'd hardly ever gone this way before, as I'd only started at the school that term, and Mum had usually driven me in on her way to the hospital in Bakewell where she works. All the year elevens had to go to either Bakewell or Sheffield; miles away, both of them. We spent hours travelling to and from school every day. But at least the bus would have taken me all the way there, and I would have sat near Caroline. Trust me to go and miss it! I knew it meant that I had to walk all the way to Edale station, wait forty minutes and take a train to Hope, walk half a mile to the stop, then wait forever for a bus to take me to Bakewell. What a pain! Later, I realised that I could have gone home and phoned up to say I'd got flu; I never even thought of that. All I thought about then was seeing Caroline.

By the time I arrived at school it was the end of break, I was in trouble, and I'd missed the only lesson I shared with Caroline. But none of that was as bad as the nagging sense of unease I felt all day about Win Lingworth.

2

The more I thought about her, the better I remembered her; a white-haired, clever-looking little woman. I had only seen her once, on the station platform, pacing up and down when Mum and I were waiting for the train one day. It was a few years ago. We hadn't lived in Edale very long and Mum was anxious to get to know people in the valley.

"Are you local?" Mum asked her.

I shrank into the draughty brick cupboard that serves as a waiting room. It embarrasses me, the way Mum will talk to just about anyone. As long as she doesn't introduce me, it's not so bad. I'm never sure whether I have to shake hands or not, and my big fear is that I might hold my hand out and the other person doesn't even see it. So I usually pretend I don't belong, or I've found something interesting on the floor, or better still, that I don't even exist.

"I am." The woman had answered rather stiffly, as if she resented the intrusion into her silence. Mum said later that she thought it was shyness, but then, Mum always thinks the best of everyone.

"Ah, I'm pleased to meet you. I'm Sandra Parker, and this is my son, Shaun. So hard to get to know people. You are —?"

"Win Lingworth." She treated Mum to a surprisingly sweet, dimpled smile, then edged away as if she was peering to see if the train was coming through the distant tunnel. One head-lamp means it'll stop here, two means it's the express from Manchester to Sheffield. You can stand for hours on this platform, never knowing whether you're late for the train, or you've missed it, or if it's been cancelled altogether. And when it does come, it either flies past without stopping or it's such ancient rolling stock that you think it's going to die on you before it reaches the platform.

"Off to Sheffield?" Oh, Mum is so nosy when she's trying to be friendly.

Miss Lingworth took a deep breath, obviously resigning herself to conversation. "Yes. I'm going on to London."

"Nice."

"I hate London." Miss Lingworth paced a bit further away from us.

"So you're not going to see the sights."

Silence for a beat or two.

"Is it a business trip?"

"I have a meeting with my research assistant."

"Oh?" Mum's question marks throbbed in the air like little dragonflies, and at last Miss Lingworth satisfied her.

"I'm a writer," giving the briefest of smiles this time. Then she tilted her glasses at Mum, putting a final glassy barrier between them; a 'Don't ask me anything else' sort of look, and moved off to the other end of the platform.

Mum couldn't wait to find out more. She phoned one of her friends, Cindy, who used to be headmistress of the village primary school and knew just about everybody, and found out that Win Lingworth lived somewhere near the railway cutting down our end of the valley. That evening, Mum took Buster for a walk down there, just for a look. She calls it getting to know the neighbourhood. I call it spying.

"Lovely old cottage, gorgeous garden. Very secluded," she told me later. "I wouldn't choose to live there, not on my own."

So, all I knew about Win Lingworth was that she was a writer. Not very successful, by the look of her dowdy little cottage. It didn't quite fit Mum's description of it, anyway; certainly not the garden. Gorgeous jungle, more like.

I fretted about her most of the evening. I think that cheerful greeting from the farmer had unnerved me, which was why I'd been so jittery at the cottage. Why on earth shouldn't she go for a walk and leave the door open? Who was likely to intrude, round here? I tried to distract myself but as usual there was nothing to watch on telly and my DVDs had all become about as interesting as last week's weather forecast. The house seemed huge and creepy, the minutes stretched like hours. I wished Buster was there.

She was always good for a laugh. I brought my bike in and took it to bits on the kitchen floor. Mum would love that. I got so absorbed in cleaning it that I jumped like a startled rabbit when the phone rang. It was Mum, anxious to know how I was getting on without her and Buster. I told her I hadn't even noticed they weren't in the house. I looked round happily at the dissected bike on the floor.

Then, because she was obviously on the point of asking whether I'd had a good day at school, I told her about the purse and the jacket and the empty cottage.

"She'd probably just gone for a stroll," Mum said. "Hardly anybody locks their doors round here. We're townies still, that's why we do it. I'd give her a ring, Shaun. She'll be in the phone book. Just let her know you called."

It was a good idea, but it didn't help at all. It made things worse. I found Win Lingworth's number and then hesitated, cradling the phone in the palm of my hand, rehearsing what I would say. I wished I hadn't gone into her house, like an intruder. Why hadn't I just left her things on the doorstep? When at last I keyed the number the phone rang and rang for ages, and I was about to give up when she picked up the receiver. Either that or the ansaphone clicked on, it was hard to tell. Either way, no one spoke. Not a word. But I was sure I could hear someone breathing, very light, very quick, at the other end.

"Miss Lingworth," I said. "Miss Lingworth, are you there? It's Shaun Parker. I think I found some of your things."

Nothing.

I felt silly, talking to nothing. And I felt a bit scared too. So I put the phone down and stared at it for about ten minutes then went to bed.

But didn't sleep. What if it was Miss Lingworth on the other end, but she was too ill to speak? Maybe I should ring the police. But it sounded feeble. Someone didn't come to the door when I knocked. Someone didn't answer when I spoke on the phone. So what?

"She's a recluse," I told myself at last. "She likes her privacy. She has a right to it."

And I fell into an uneasy sleep.

As soon as I woke up the next morning I knew I would have to go back to the hidden cottage. I would say I wanted to make sure that the things I had found belonged to her. That was fair enough — if they weren't hers, they would have to be reported to the police. So, quite confidently this time, I set off for the track by the cutting. As I approached it I heard someone whistling a bright, chirpy tune, and just where the two tracks forked I saw a woman bending over some bushes. She looked up sharply as I drew along-side her, as if she'd been concentrating on something and I'd made her jump out of her skin. She obviously wasn't expecting anyone to come down that track. Her lips were purple blotches in a white, startled face.

"Oops," she said, smiling garishly. "Oh, it's only you, Shaun."

It's unnerving in this valley, how all the adults seem to know all the kids. They all come to the primary school play, like an extended family of doting aunts and uncles, although there's hardly ever more than twenty-two children in the school. Mind you, there's not that much else in the way of entertainment round here. Anyway, I just treated her to my best 'fancy seeing you here' smile. She picked up a bag and scuttled away from me, whistling carelessly. But it wasn't Win Lingworth, I knew that at least. It was someone from the mill cottages, though I hadn't a clue what her name was. I jogged on down the shadowy track and through the gate. The binoculars were still there. Again, the front door was open. Again, I called and knocked. Again, no answer.

I went round the back. The kitchen door was still open. I knocked and called, and again there was no answer. I took a deep breath, and stepped inside. It was a dark little kitchen, with its big, black, old-fashioned fireplace, and I was struck again by the strange modern style of the table and chairs. They didn't go with the room at all. There was that rusty, fuggy smell still. The jacket and purse and phone lay on the table, exactly where I had left them. My heart was knocking in my chest now. Something was wrong, something was desperately wrong. I would have to search the house for her. But the thought of going through the rooms, climbing the stairs, opening doors into private rooms, and finding — what? A dead woman slumped over a telephone? — was all more than I could handle. Perhaps I should look round the garden first, and then knock again, and then go away and phone the police. They could do the searching; that was their job, they were used to it.

3

I went back out into the garden, and there she was, standing in the middle of the overgrown veg. patch digging up potatoes with a rusty old fork. How come I hadn't seen her before?

"Miss Lingworth?"

"Ah, hello there!" she called. "Was it you who brought my things back? Very kind of you."

She bustled towards me, dimpling with smiles. I was so relieved that I almost hugged her.

"You've helped me a great deal, young man, more than you think," she said, pulling off her gardening gloves. Her hands had those little brown blotches that old people get. She took off her glasses and blew a speck of soil off the lens. "Ha! Can see you now. Come inside and have a cup of tea."

Of course I was overjoyed by her kind invitation, but luckily I had a good excuse. "I need to get off and catch the school bus," I told her. "I just wanted to make sure —." It sounded silly now, but she finished the sentence off for me.

"That I'm still alive? Well, I am, as you can see." Her glasses flashed merry sunshine at me. "Sorry to put you to such trouble, but you've very kindly helped me in my research. I'm writing a bit of a thriller at the moment, a murder mystery, just a silly amateur thing; I like to do a bit of scribbling. I thought I could set it here. This would be a beautiful place for a murder, don't you think? I laid a kind of trap for you, I'm afraid. Just wanted to see what would happen if someone found a purse and a jacket and an empty house. I can move on to the next bit now. Very exciting! I might make you one of the characters!"

She beamed at me so cheerfully that it was hard to be angry with her, but my relief had turned to embarrassment and more than a slight annoyance. I thought she'd made a fool of me, and now I just wanted to get away and forget the whole silly business. I turned to move off.

"Wait a minute," she called. "I want to give you something for your honesty and your help." She dived into the kitchen.

"No, I really don't want anything," I called. "I'd better be off."

She emerged quickly with a bottle of something pink. "Strawberry wine," she said. "You're old enough to drink wine, I'm sure. It's homemade, and it's the last one. Beautiful, isn't it? Look at the colour." She held it up so the sun was shining through it, giving it a pale pink glow like roses. She held it out to me. "Take it," she said, "with my sincere thanks."

"Thank you." I hate wine, but I was too embarrassed to say so. I stuffed the bottle awkwardly into my schoolbag and turned away.

"Make sure you drink it all yourself!" she called. "And come back to see me any time you like!"

I ran for the bus, the wine slurping in its bottle. Maybe something good would come of it, after all. I would show it to Caroline, I promised myself. I'd invite her round, and we'd share it. And then, oh bliss, and then —

I missed the bus. And German, which was the only lesson I shared with Caroline. I didn't see her to speak to all day, but I did notice her chatting to Tom Hemsley at lunchtime. He lives in Edale, he's over a year older than I am, he's probably the best-looking kid in school, and he's just passed his driving test. First time. Well, I like Tom, every one does, he's the only person who can beat the vicar at tennis, for a start, but I felt so annoyed with him for the way Caroline was glowing at him that I wanted to trip him up when he walked past. He was probably inviting her out for a drive. Passing your test is *the* status symbol round here. In Edale, the farm kids learn to drive when they're about ten, charging up and down the fields on massive tractors or little red quads, rounding up the sheep. The rest of the kids start learning on their seventeenth birthday on the dot, so their parents have to stop ferrying them round the county. That must be an awful disappointment to the adults, but they learn to do something else with their time. I still had a year to go before I could get my provisional licence. It felt like a lifetime.

So, back home to my bike bits. Someone had left a carton of eggs on the doorstep, without a note, but I assumed Mum had asked Geoff, the farmer next door, to deliver them. He keeps little bantams that look like feather dusters and cock-a-doodle every five minutes. Buster's terrified of them. The eggs are the size of cherry tomatoes but they taste fantastic. They weren't bantam eggs, as it turned out, but they were still farm-yard dusty and had neat little feathers stuck to them with hen shit. That was good then. Mum and I won't touch shop eggs. We can't bear the thought of rows of hens in tiny cages on factory shelves, producing eggs as if they were little machines. How can anyone do that to a live animal?

I decided to be really adventurous and make an omelette. The house was so loud with the silence of no Mum and no Buster that I put on a CD at maximum volume, sang my head off, and danced over the bike bits while I chopped several onions and a bit of cauliflower into the omelette, burned it, scrambled it, and finally scraped it onto a plate. The inside of the frying pan looked like a totally brilliant piece of abstract art.

I hardly heard the phone when it rang. It was someone asking if I'd enjoyed the eggs and had I by any chance found something or other that I couldn't hear. It was a woman's voice, but I couldn't place it over the dulcet tones of the Arctic Monkeys. Probably one of Mum's reading group friends wanting to borrow the latest book on the list in exchange for the non-bantie eggs. We shouted at each other for a bit and then whoever it was gave up and put down the receiver. The CD stopped, I finished my egg mess, put the abstract art in the sink, and the long silent evening stretched in front of me like a prison sentence.

I didn't see Caroline again till the next day. I managed to sit behind her on the bus, and to my joy she actually turned round to speak to me.

Yes, her eyes are blue.

"I've got some German notes for you, but I've left them at home."

My chance had come, and I grabbed it with grateful hands.

"Could you bring them round tonight?" I asked innocently. "I'd come round to yours, but I've got to wait for a phone call from Mum."

That was true, but there was nothing wrong with our ansaphone. She gave me one of those bone-melting smiles and whispered something to the girl sitting next to her, and I rode on a cloud all the way to school.

When I got home that night I pushed the bike bits under the kitchen table, had a go at scrubbing the abstract art and sorted out some good CDs. I put the bottle of strawberry wine on the kitchen windowsill so the evening light shone through it. Caroline noticed it as soon as she came in.

"It's so beautiful," she said. "As if the sunset is inside it."

"I want to share it with you," I said. "Shall we

have some now?" My hand was reaching for the corkscrew, and shaking a little. My mind was already thinking about later, later. But she smiled and shook her head.

"I can't," she said. "Mum's waiting outside for me. We're going to Sheffield. I need some reference books from the central library."

I must have looked as crestfallen as I felt, because she put the German notes on the table and then touched my hand, light and cool as a snowflake, and I felt delicious electric shocks running up and down me. I don't know whether she did it deliberately or not. I wanted to put my hand over hers, but daren't. When we were kids and our mums used to get together to talk about their old university days, Caroline and I used to scrap a lot, pushing each other over and jumping on each other like a pair of puppies. Now I hardly even dared stand next to her. I wanted to touch her all the time, I couldn't stop thinking about her. Was it the same for her, or was I just like an annoying brother? And then the phone rang, and my mum was on for ages raving about the fact that she'd just seen a herd of wild deer, and then Caroline's mum was hooting outside the gate. Caroline looked at me helplessly, and the electric shocks started all over again.

"Come with us," she said. "Pretend you've got to go to the library too."

I'd have gone with her if she'd been driving to the rubbish tip.

It was while I was waiting for her and her mother to come out of the central library that I saw Win Lingworth again. She was crossing the road to the underpass that led down to the Sheffield Interchange. I raised my hand to wave to her but she didn't see me, or didn't want to see me. She was hurrying, and her face looked grim, and white, and ugly. There was definitely something different about her, but I couldn't put my finger on it. It wasn't just her expression, either. It made me feel cold with unease. Caroline came out of the library just then and I pointed her out.

"There's Win Lingworth," I said. "From the hidden cottage."

Caroline shook her head. "I don't think that's her," she said. "Win's hair's different, I'm sure. Thicker than that."

"So you know her?"

"Mum does, a bit," Caroline said. "In fact, she and I met her on the lane a few weeks ago; I think she'd been walking down from Hollins Cross. Mum offered her a lift but she turned it down. I don't think anyone knows her well. She doesn't mix. But I'm sure that's not her."

So, I was mistaken. But I couldn't get her out of my mind; the whole strange business was haunting me.

When we were driving back home I told Caroline and her mum the story about the strawberry wine. Her mother was very amused.

"I'm pleased to know she's turning to thrillers," she said. "She writes very stuffy books about international politics. Your mum and I looked her up on the Internet one day. Very high up in her field, by all accounts."

"The strawberry wine's still waiting," I whispered to Caroline as I climbed out of the car at our gate. "How about tomorrow?"

She just shook her head and gave me a smile that was half-rueful and half-teasing. "Away," she mouthed.

I found out when I was on the school bus next morning that Caroline was on a field trip, staying overnight on a campsite somewhere near Stanton Moor. Lucky campers, lucky tent, lucky sleeping bag. I was as miserable as a soggy dog all day. It was my last chance of having that evening of bliss. When I got home the house was empty and quiet; no Mum, no Buster, no Caroline. I took Miss Lingworth's bottle of strawberry wine and held it up to the light. It looked as if it was glowing with secrets. I could still hear Caroline's voice saying, "It's so beautiful. As if the sunset is inside it."

I would drink to that, I decided. I would drink to me and Caroline, and the sunset; I would drown my sorrows. I fished around for the angel corkscrew and was about to open the bottle when I realised what a saddo I would be, drinking on my own, drinking wine of all things, which I loved about as much as vinegar without the chips. I put the bottle back on the windowsill. I'd give it to Mum tomorrow. That's what I'd do. A welcome home present.

I went out for a run instead. The bats were out, black scraps of rag dive-bombing the midges. I couldn't resist jogging down towards Miss Lingworth's. It was true, she was haunting me. I was just turning past the two wheelie bins at the end of her lane when a car horn tooted, making my bones nearly jump out of my skin. Molly Oldroyd, the oldest woman in Edale, was driving her Fiesta straight at me. That's another thing about driving in Edale. Not only can you start when you're ten but you carry on till you're at least ninety-four. On Molly's ninetieth birthday the villagers clubbed together to get her car through its test, to keep her mobile. She peered at me and wound down her window, driving alongside me as I was running.

"Are you managing all right on your own? Want any more eggs?"

Ah, so it was her little present. How did she know Mum was away?

"No thanks Molly. Still cleaning the pan," I puffed.

"And I'm still looking for my whatsits! Such a nuisance! Can't manage without them." She swerved round a crow that was tugging a rabbit carcass off the road, and I jammed myself into the hedge, just managing to save my life. The hawthorn branches closed round me like an army of hedgehogs. I smiled gratefully at her as she careered on her way, and picked myself out of the hedge.

I plunged down into the safety of Miss Lingworth's track. I would jog up to the house and back again. If I saw her, I'd thank her for the wine. I'd tell her it was delicious. I'd ask her how her thriller was coming on. I stopped at the gate, panting, noting that she'd retrieved the binoculars at last. It was quite late now. Sheep coughed on the hillside. The sudden *crack*! of a farmer's shotgun echoed off the rocks, sending a clatter of crows up. The drone of insects was as heavy as a distant rumble of thunder. And in Miss Lingworth's kitchen, silence; utter, utter silence.

An open door, a silent, empty house, and day breathing towards night. Long grey shadows. Under the trees, pipistrelles darting like tiny black missiles. I couldn't get home fast enough.

4

After that, I couldn't wait for Mum and Buster to come home. I'd had enough of being on my own. It was turning my imagination loopy. And now that Caroline was away there was nothing much to look forward to — more past-their-sell-by date CDs, more delicious home cooking, more crusty washing-up. If only Caroline hadn't been away on that field trip, we could have made great progress. As it was, I wrote letters to her that never got sent — how do you send a letter to a tent? Mobiles don't work at our end of Edale, so they wouldn't work up on Stanton Moor. The atmosphere would probably be spooked by the stone circle. And protestors sleep up in the trees round there to stop the local quarry being extended; they certainly wouldn't allow a phone mast to be put up in their sacred place. She could have phoned me on our landline, but she didn't. She might as well have been on the moon. I couldn't get her smile, or the sound of her voice, or the blue sky of her eyes out of my mind. Well, it was better to be haunted by Caroline than by Miss Lingworth, anyway.

And something else was happening. Because I couldn't sleep, every night since Mum went away I heard the low throb of a tractor prowling up and down, up and down on the hillside, in the moonlight. How spooky was that?

As soon as I heard Mum's Skoda I was out in the lane, waving to her. She was as pleased to see me as I was to see her. Buster came leaping out of the car and licked me all over as if I needed a bath, then bounced into the kitchen and nearly knocked the bottle of wine off the table. I rescued it just in time, and handed it to Mum.

"Welcome home."

"How lovely!" said Mum. "What an amazing colour. Strawberry wine!"

I held it up so she could see the light shining through it. "It looks as if it's got the sunset inside it." It sounded a bit pompous when I said it. I whisked two glasses out of the cupboard. "Let's have some now."

"No, not just yet," she said. "I really could do with a walk, and so could Buster, after that long drive. You could make a bicycle out of those bits under the table, by the way. Come with me and tell me all the news, and when we come back, we'll open the bottle and celebrate."

But the bottle was never opened, thanks to Mum's curiosity and Buster's passion for water.

As we walked I told Mum about Win Lingworth — well, it was the only news I had. Mum was fascinated.

"Let's go there now," she said. "I'd love to meet her properly."

"She hides," I warned her. "There's something really strange about that place. It's so quiet. It's eerie."

"She needs friends, that's all. It's too easy to be isolated here; you have to work at it if you want to meet people. I know what I'll do. I'll ask her if she'd like to donate a couple of bottles of her beautiful wine to the local products stall in the Autumn Fair."

"It's her last bottle," I argued weakly. I knew that Mum wouldn't give up now she knew that Miss Lingworth was writing a thriller, especially as I was apparently going to have a star part in it. It certainly made her a bit more interesting. Political analysis wasn't quite Mum's thing. I wasn't even sure what it meant myself.

"I could invite her to give a talk to the WI." Mum rattled on, confirming my suspicions absolutely. "We haven't had a writer for a few years."

Buster lolloped ahead of us down the midgy track, and then stopped suddenly, snarling and crouching in a strange, cowed way. She didn't want to go any further, and to tell the truth, neither did I. And we arrived to the same eerie stillness, the open front door, the open kitchen door, the jacket and purse still on the table, the terrible ceaseless droning of flies. And then Buster noticed the pond and flung herself straight in, and disturbed what I had thought from the distance of the kitchen step was a dark jumble of weeds.

No, it wasn't.
It was a body.
It was Win Lingworth.

5

Mum phoned the police from our house, and we sat in anxious, unbelieving silence waiting to see what would happen next. We couldn't eat, either of us. The bottle of strawberry wine stayed where it was on the table, a grim reminder of our awful find. It was a relief when the police car arrived, lighting up our room with its head-lamps. Only then did we realise that we had been sitting without the lights on, and it had gone dark outside.

Inspector Philip refused Mum's half-hearted offer of a cup of tea. He was a big, burly man, so tall that he had to stoop to come through into the kitchen. I've scraped my hair a few times on the beams, but I'm a long way from banging my head. He was with a younger man who looked as if he was into extreme sports. They told us that they would have to question us both as we were witnesses, and that we would have to be inter-viewed separately. The sporty one went with Mum into the living room. The Inspector told me that as I was only sixteen he would have to wait for an appropriate adult to come and sit with me while we talked, so a social worker was on her way. Of course she got lost; people always do when they're coming to our house. Nobody believes that anyone actually lives up our lane. Buster padded anxiously between the living room and the kitchen. She knew something was up.

While we were waiting, the Inspector took two phone calls. He replied in monosyllables, so it was impossible to know what the calls were about, but after the second one he went into the dining room where Mum was being interviewed and whispered something to the other policeman. I could see Mum leaning back in the sofa, tired, like me.

The appropriate adult arrived at last, full of apologies. She didn't look at all appropriate to me, considering we were going to be talking about someone who'd just died. I kept catching shimmers of a sparkly dress under her coat, and scenting drifts of spiky perfume. Her lipstick was like a crimson scar in a too-white face.

"I was on my way to a party," she told us. "I wish you could have found someone else."

"Sorry to spoil your evening," the Inspector rumbled. I didn't think that was very appropriate, either.

"Half-past ten," I muttered.

"I know you're tired and upset, young man, but we'll just have a little chat and then you can go off to bed. Just a few routine questions."

The questions took ages; ages and ages. I couldn't think straight, I kept correcting myself. He wanted to know exactly how and when Mum and I had found Miss Lingworth, and why we had gone to the cottage that evening. Then he wanted to know about the last time I'd seen Miss Lingworth, was anyone else there, what was she doing, what did she say, how did she seem, what was she wearing? I haven't a clue what she was wearing.

"Try to remember. It's important."

His eyebrows bristled. The appropriate adult stretched her jagged scar into some sort of sympathetic smile. Buster whined.

"It wasn't the jacket I'd found, because that was still in her kitchen," I said for the sake of saying something.

"So you went into her kitchen?"

"Sort of. I don't think I went in." The door had been open. Did I look through it, or did I go inside? I couldn't remember.

"It's all right," the Inspector said. "Take your time. I'm in no hurry, and Miss Watson's given up on her party by now. Tell me again about those objects you found. Can you describe them?"

And so it went on, while the green clock on the cooker jumped on from minute to minute. I did remember some things very clearly. I remembered Win Lingworth's bright, cheerful smile when she gave me her precious last bottle of wine. I remembered the scary, breathing silence at the end of the ansaphone. But the more I said about my actual reason for going to her cottage in the first place, the less convincing it seemed.

"So you found a purse, then a jacket with the mobile phone in the pocket, and then binoculars hanging by the gate. You say she dropped them all."

"She'd set a little trap for me," I told him.

He nodded and glanced at his watch. I could sense that he wasn't impressed with this part of the story. I was doing my best. I wanted to be as helpful as I could; after all, I had nothing to hide. The questions had been quite interesting at first, but now I was tired and confused. It was like taking an oral exam at school; however well you know the answers, you still get blurry-brained.

"She said she was writing a thriller."

He nodded again.

I knew what he was thinking. It all sounded as limp as a fish's handshake.

"Were they still there?" I asked. "The things I found. On the table?"

He pursed his lips into a 'don't ask me,' sort of face. We fell into a drowsy silence. He was watching me under his bristly eyebrows. The appropriate adult made that kind of huffing noise behind her hand that you make when you're stifling a yawn. I was expected to speak, and I couldn't think of a thing to say. But the things on the table must have gone, I was thinking. Surely he'd ask me to identify them if they were still there. Were they important? Did he think I'd stolen them, or did he think I'd made them up? I hadn't a clue.

Mum's interview had finished long ago; I could tell by the natural chatter that was coming through the dining-room door. She was probably showing the policeman all the family photographs by now. Eventually she knocked on the door and offered tea. I felt more relaxed then. I'd got used to the kitchen with all these strangers in it; which was why I started offering suggestions.

"What if she had a heart attack when she was in her garden," I went, "and she was phoning for help on her mobile and she staggered into the pond with it?" And then I just wiped out my brilliant suggestion. "Ah no. She couldn't have used her mobile, could she?"

"Exactly." The Inspector sipped his tea noisily and waited for me to make my next attempt.

"She might have been using her binoculars!" I had an image of Miss Lingworth scanning the sky for a heron or a sparrow hawk or something, stepping backwards and — splash! — floundering helplessly in the water. "Maybe you should search the pond for them," I suggested.

"You don't have to tell us our job, young man." I think he was tired too. His voice was getting crabby. He finished his tea and went on with his questions.

So, hours later it seemed, the policemen left, Miss Watson repaired her make-up and went off to her party, and I went to bed. I thought I'd gone up without eating anything but Mum told me next day that I'd eaten five rounds of toast and jam, posting them in my mouth one after another and practically swallowing them whole. I don't remember any of that.

But I couldn't sleep. How could I? I would never forget the sight of that hump of clothing in the pond, never ever forget the horror of leaning over it and seeing a face, the face of Win Lingworth, in the gloomy green weeds. The moon in the trees flickered like water on my bedroom ceiling, and out on the hillside the night ghost tractor moaned like the hum of insects.

6

Mum and I were as jumpy as cats the next day, so we walked over to the post office just to give ourselves something to do. There would be nearly a week's supply of *The Guardian* to pick up, because I'd completely forgotten to collect it for Mum every day. We could have gone over the fields but instead, without even discussing it, we went along the lane, even though it would take us past the track that led to Miss Lingworth's. I think we were both morbidly drawn to the place, as if we wanted to keep an eye on it, take care of it; not that we would have dreamt of going anywhere near the cottage itself. Two policemen were standing by the wheelie bins. They nodded to us affably.

"Lovely morning," one of them said.

How could they even notice what kind of day it was?

"Why are they there?" I asked Mum. "I thought it was all over with by now." It made me think what a strange job it was, a policeman's, when fishing a dead woman out of a pond was all part of a day's work.

"I think they have to stay there while the house is being searched."

"That farmer will be thrilled to bits."

39

"Joe Eldridge?"

"He loves company."

A bit later I made myself ask, "Why would they need to search the house anyway?"

"To establish the cause of death."

"But surely it's obvious."

"Nothing's obvious."

I brooded over that as we walked along. Blurry-brained though I was with lack of sleep, I surprised myself with a sudden fizz of excitement as I imagined telling Caroline about all this. I thought of her eyes, blue and brimming with astonishment.

"Not Miss Lingworth? Dead, in her own pond! How awful! And you *found* her! Were you scared, Shaun?"

"Me? No. Not a bit."

When we reached the village we could see a little crowd of gossips, the usual suspects, the elders of Edale, hanging about outside the post office. Usually I wonder what on earth they found to talk about.

"Shaun, don't mention the fact that we were the ones who found Win Lingworth," Mum said.

"Why not?" I was mystified. What did it matter who found her?

"Just don't. Not till it's all over."

So we nodded our way past the female chorus and into the post office, where Jane the postmistress asked us if the police had been to see us yet. Her hands dithered with excitement as she shuffled Mum's papers into a pile.

"Well," Mum began, but Jane didn't wait for an answer.

"They will. You have heard, haven't you? About poor Win Lingworth? The place is swarming with policemen, doing door to door enquiries. It's not just the local C.I.D, either. Everyone's being asked when they last saw her. Trouble is, most people don't even know who she is, and those who do can't remember when they last saw her. I certainly can't. She used to call in quite regularly with stuff to post, and to buy a few groceries, but she hasn't been in for months and months. Gets her food delivered from a supermarket in Buxton, I believe."

She dumped Mum's *Guardians* on the counter.

"The only person who sees her regularly would be Jenny the postie," she said. "I told the police that. Ask the postie. She sees everything that happens round here."

We actually met Jenny delivering our post just as we arrived home. She bustled straight into the story.

"Isn't it awful? Can't say I knew her well, but I liked her. If ever I had something to deliver there, which wasn't often, books usually, or manuscripts from London, she used to give me a cheery wave through the window or from her garden. She was a happy woman. Know what I mean? Content with her life, liked her own company. But she did

41

change recently. Seemed to lose interest in the garden. I thought that was strange, because she used to tell me that gardening helped her to think. She kept out of my way, and just ignored me if she saw me. One day she left me a note to stop delivering mail, as it was all junk anyway. And she was right. Those important–looking packages she used to get stopped coming, and so I hardly went any more. Left the junk in a box she'd put out down by the wheelie bins — she probably chucked them straight into the bin, but that's not my problem. I used to have a little rest near her place though, after I'd delivered to Joe's. It's about halfway through my round, so I have my cup of coffee from my flask. It's a lovely spot. And I never, ever see anyone going to her house."

She handed Mum a bunch of letters rolled inside an elastic band. "Except you, of course, Shaun. I have to say I've seen you going there recently. I had to tell the police that, of course. But I'm sure you had a very good reason to go to her house."

And she swung her postbag over her shoulder and marched away before I'd had a chance to answer her.

Mum shut the door carefully behind her. She looked worried, really white and worried. I wasn't exactly feeling full of cheer myself.

"We'd better stay here," she said. "It won't surprise me if the police want to question you again, Shaun. So I might as well stay in and paint the bathroom."

Buster moaned. No more long walks for her, then. I phoned Caroline, but only got her dad's rather formal ansaphone message, and because I couldn't think of anything to say, I said nothing. I sat outside putting my bike together again, trying to keep myself sane, but by late morning the younger policeman came round again and said they wanted to see me back at the station.

Mum ran downstairs at once, paint brush in hand. She'd managed to flick paint all over herself. Jitters, probably. "Why has he got to go?" Her voice was shrill and nervous, not Mum's voice at all. "He's already told you as much as he knows."

"We want to ask a few more questions," the policeman said. "And we want to take his finger-prints."

"I'd better get this paint off my face," Mum said.

"You won't be needed. Shaun will be given a video interview, he'll be fine. Miss Watson will be there again. He'll be brought home later."

"All the same, I'd like to come with him. He's never been in any trouble." Mum glanced at me, and I could just see the word 'before' hovering on her lips. I felt that she was the one who needed protecting, not me. She was doing her best to be brave, I could tell.

"We want you to stay here. A policewoman will be round to talk to you again this afternoon, so please stay at home."

"I think I have a right to know," Mum insisted. "Is this a murder enquiry?"

The policeman said nothing, just tightened his lips, and jerked his head at me to get in the car.

7

Miss Watson was waiting for me at the police station, her face looking a little late-night-party stained, but dressed in appropriate clothes this time. She followed me into the Inspector's room and sat with her eyes closed, as if she was trying to catch up on her sleep.

As soon as he came in, Inspector Philip started with the same round of questions. Every time I recounted the story of the trail of objects and my meeting with Miss Lingworth in her garden, it sounded more and more feeble. The Inspector didn't accuse me of lying, but he didn't believe me, I could sense it.

"Why do you keep asking me these things?" I asked at last, exhausted and frustrated. If I could drag more truth out of thin air, I would have done. "Do you always ask questions like this, when someone drowns?"

He said nothing, just watched me. A long, silent moment ticked by, and in that moment I felt murky waters sliding round me, I felt myself turning and floating slowly, slowly to the surface, to the pale yellow light of a winter sun. And the truth, the slow horrible truth, dawned on me.

"She didn't drown, did she? She was already dead!"

"What makes you say that?" the Inspector asked, sharp as a flick-knife. "What do you mean?"

I covered my face with my hands. The video camera was on me, I knew that. Everything I said, everything I did, was recorded for all time and open to scrutiny. The yellow sun was eclipsed. I was falling into a deep, dark well of suspicion. "What do *you* mean? What's it got to do with me? Why don't you believe what I'm telling you?"

"Why don't you tell me the truth?"

"I am!" My voice flicked into falsetto, something it hasn't done since I was fourteen.

"A few things are worrying us. We have found the purse, which you say you found in the road. We want to match up the fingerprints, for a start."

"Of course mine will be on it," I shouted. "I found it, didn't I?"

The Inspector tutted like a granddad and told me it wasn't helpful to lose my temper. It looked very bad for me, he said. At least he didn't call me Shane, like they do on those TV detective dramas. They always get the name wrong, as if that's a way of putting you down. Actually, he didn't call me anything.

"Ask Mum," I told him. "She knows. She phoned me on Monday and I told her then about finding the purse."

"I know," said the Inspector. He was being friendly again, reassuring. I knew what that meant. They had what they wanted. They practically had a confession. Miss Lingworth was already dead when she was put into the pond. Who would know that better than the person who put her there? Why did I have to say that?

"We just have to make sure you haven't forgotten anything. Some of the facts don't fit, and we're trying to understand why. This is a very important enquiry."

"A murder enquiry," I murmured, feeling utterly wretched. It was one thing to have a part in a little murder mystery story. It had sounded as if it might be good fun. It was something else altogether to be caught up in the horrible reality of the actual thing.

"Nobody has said anything about that," Inspector Philip reminded me.

"It is though, isn't it?"

He didn't deny it. "We're just investigating all possibilities. Let's try again. Did you see anyone else near the cottage on any of your visits there?"

I sighed. I wished I could think of something new to tell him. "Yes. I already told you, I was shouted at by a farmer. All I did was open his gate, and he roared at me like a bull. I saw a woman hiding behind a bush just up the lane from the road — she had a purple mouth. And another day I saw Molly by the wheelie bins — she's ninety-four and she was driving as if she was on a race-track."

47

I was being as helpful as I could with my descriptions. The Inspector raised his eyebrows, which looked as if they'd been knitted out of Brillo pads, and repeated it all slowly.

"And you've never been there before?"

I shook my head. "Never in my life. I told you. I went once to take the things I'd found. I went back to see if they were hers. I went once with my mum."

"Three times."

"That's what I said."

"Wrong," he said. "Count again."

Miss Watson leaned forward, interested now.

"Three times," I repeated sullenly. I gave him the exact dates, the exact times. What more did he want? What more could I say?

"You were seen near the cottage by two independent witnesses three days before any of those visits. How do you explain that?"

There was a long, puzzled silence. He pushed his chair back with a shriek that made Miss Watson jump. She smiled apologetically. He walked over to the window and dipped a slit in the Venetian blinds with his little finger, as if he was trying to see whether it was still daylight out there in that other world where I used to live.

"OK," he said at last, abruptly, as if he was bored of me. "Off you go. But stay at home or nearby till you hear from us again."

"What about school on Monday?"

"We'll let you know." He was inscrutable.

"I hope I've been of some assistance, Inspector." It probably sounded sarcastic because I was so fed up, but I meant it. I really wanted to be as helpful as I possibly could. But the awful truth was beginning to dawn on me; if they found that Win Lingworth had been murdered, then I was probably the chief suspect.

It was on the local television news that night; a sixty-year-old reclusive woman writer had been found dead in her pond. The circumstances of death were suspicious. There was a shot of her cottage with the reporter standing in front of it. We see him every night when we're eating our tea. His face was so familiar that if I'd seen him walking down the lane I'd have greeted him like an uncle. "It appears that Win Lingworth had been in the pond for at least a week before her body was found," he said, checking his notes.

"A *week*!" I looked at Mum in a panic. How could this be true? I counted back — I had found the things on Monday, met her on Tuesday, and we found her body on Friday. "That doesn't add up!"

"Ssh! Let's listen."

I was still counting days on my fingers when I heard the reporter saying that a sixteen-year-old boy, who could not be named, thank God, had been helping the police with their enquiries. There was no mention of anyone else.

Joe Eldridge, the farmer who had shouted at me for opening his gate, was shown standing in the lane shaking his head in disbelief. He looked as if he hadn't slept for a week, and his face was stubbled like a newly cut hayfield. "Well, she were a quiet soul, kept hersen to hersen. To tell you truth, I hardly ever saw her from one year end to next. Why anyone should want to do her harm, I don't know. I hope they catch him soon. It's frightened wits out of my wife. She won't come near farm now, not till he's found." His voice trembled as he spoke; that same voice that had bellowed at me like a bull with a headache, weak now with emotion.

"He looks wiped out with shock, poor man," Mum said.

"Poor him! What about me? It'll be all over the valley that I've been taken in for questioning."

"They didn't say your name."

"Mum! How many sixteen-year-old boys are there in Edale? One!"

We had a phone call from Molly Oldroyd immediately after the News. She told Mum she just wanted to send us her good wishes in our time of trouble. Because she's deaf she shouts, so I could hear every word she was saying. Mum was flustered and said she didn't know what she was talking about, to which Molly replied that I had been seen going to Miss Lingworth's cottage while Mum was away, several times, but that she had no doubt in her mind that I was innocent.

"Thank you for your concern," Mum said. "But this has nothing to do with Shaun."

"Terrible business," Molly burbled on, "and I wouldn't wish it on anyone in the world. But I have to say Win Lingworth was a very peculiar woman and in the past year or so she's just let that lovely old cottage go to wrack and ruin, in my opinion. I've written to her more than once about it. Did you have a nice holiday? I do love Windermere at this time of year when the tourists leave it to itself. So wild."

"How did she know I'd gone to The Lakes?" Mum muttered at me under the nosy flow of pleasantries, but I just shrugged and made my way upstairs, feeling as miserable as a dog with fleas. So, by now, everyone in Edale would know that I was under suspicion. Molly would make quite sure of that.

I threw myself on my bed. I felt sick. Questions nagged me like a swarm of angry bees. What if Win Lingworth had really been murdered? Why would anyone do it? How on earth could the police suspect me? All I'd done was to return some lost property. What possible motive could I have for murdering her? But how could I prove my innocence? In British law you're innocent till you're proved guilty, I reminded myself. But that wasn't true. What about those women who had been accused of killing their own babies? Just because they couldn't prove that they hadn't done it, they'd all been jailed. What about the man who'd been carrying a chair-leg in a carrier bag? They hadn't even given him a chance to prove that it wasn't a shotgun. What about the innocent Brazilian chap who the police shot in London? They didn't ask him if he was a terrorist. They shot him in the head eight times just in case. I broke into a cold sweat, just thinking about it. And then there was that strange remark that the Inspector had made, that I'd been seen near Win Lingworth's cottage days before I'd said I'd been there for the first time. Why would anyone say that, unless they were trying to frame me? And who would want to do that, except the murderer himself?

I heard someone knocking at the door downstairs and recognised voices in the kitchen. It was Caroline and her mother. They'd have seen the television news, no doubt. They'd come round to show their solidarity. But I couldn't face them. I couldn't just stroll down naturally into our kitchen and just laugh it off; I didn't know how to do it. So I stayed up in my room, not wanting to see them or talk to them, refusing to answer when my mum called to me to come down and have some tea. I sat on my bed staring at the white face in the mirror, the dark rings under my eyes, the tangle of messy hair. Did it look like the face of a murderer? It did.

Eventually Caroline came up and knocked on my door. "Shaun, can I come in?" she asked.

I choked back a sob of self-pity. Why should she want anything to do with me? I'd soon be a convicted murderer. She came in anyway and sat watching me while I blubbed into my pillow. I couldn't help it.

"You've got to believe me, Caroline. I didn't do it," I croaked.

"'Course you didn't. And nobody thinks so either. The police had to question you, of course they did, but it doesn't mean to say they think you did it."

I snuffled back a sob. "I'm sorry." I hated her to see me looking like this.

"Don't be. You can't help it, you're in delayed shock. It must have been awful for you, finding her like that."

"I've never seen a dead person before."

"Nor me. When you come to think about it, death's usually such a tidy thing, isn't it? People usually die tucked up in bed, especially if they're old. All the people we see in a day, hundreds on a school day — thousands if you live in a town, and you never see a dead one. Or a dead animal, for that matter, unless it's been run over." She shuddered. "I'd have been shocked, if I'd found her. I'd have been a total wreck. Anyway, sit up and blow your nose. God, you look disgusting. Go and wash your face while I think."

I felt better after I'd stuck my head under the cold shower. When I came back she had one of my school notebooks in her hand.

"Let's go through your story again. It's obvious that the person you met at the cottage was *not* Win Lingworth because the poor woman was dead."

"Well, I've already worked that out."

She smiled at me, and put her head to one side in a way that made her hair shiver down over her shoulders. It was hard to concentrate; it made me slip away from myself.

"You thought she looked like her though." She prompted me back to the moment. "Think, Shaun. What made you think it was her?"

I frowned. "Whoever it was, she wanted me to believe she was Win Lingworth. So I did. I've hardly ever seen her before," I reminded her. "I'd only met her once in my life. But yes, she did look like her. Little, white hair, glasses — well, I pointed her out to you. I'm still sure that was the woman I saw when we went to the library that night in Sheffield."

Caroline shook her head. "I wouldn't have mistaken her myself. OK — there was a resemblance, and I only really saw the back of her. I just had the impression of a shock of thick white hair when Mum and I met her. And I don't think that woman in town was wearing glasses. Miss Lingworth couldn't have gone anywhere without her glasses, she wore very thick lenses."

"I knew there was something different!" I said. "She *did* wear glasses when I saw her in her garden, but that day in Sheffield she wasn't wearing them. She looked at me when she was crossing the road, and her eyes were so cold that I felt odd. That's how I remember. I expected her to give me that cheery smile, and she didn't. She looked right through me."

"Well, it could still be that the woman you saw in town *was* the woman you saw at the cottage."

"It was," I nodded. "Deffo."

"OK. Let's say it was." She took a deep breath. "In which case, let's carry on thinking. So, it wasn't Miss Lingworth, because she was already dead. But who was it? Win Lingworth could have had a sister, I suppose, who looked like her. How could we find out?"

"I wonder if there's anything about her background on the Internet. That's how Mum found out she was a writer."

"Worth a try." Caroline switched on my computer and Googled on Win Lingworth. Surprisingly, there were several pages about her. Most of them were entries in academic journals. She seemed to have won some important major award a couple of years ago, and there was an entry in *The Times,* a photograph of her with a bunch of over-dressed people. 'I owe everything to Phyllis. She's such a support.' Win Lingworth had said, unsmiling in the centre, holding a medal. I couldn't take my eyes off that photograph.

Caroline Googled on. There was a lot of stuff; articles about her, as well as by her. 'Winifred Lingworth, a major political analyst, an astonishing intelligence,' one of the headlines said.

I leaned over Caroline's shoulder and clicked back to that line-up of luminaries at the award ceremony. "I wonder who on earth Phyllis is. This must be significant — 'I owe everything to Phyllis'."

"The sister, perhaps?"

Caroline printed out the photograph and handed it to me. I stared at it, feeling strangely cold. I put it down. "What if her award was for something she'd written to expose some political despot, and he'd sent an agent to take his revenge?"

"That sort of thing does happen," Caroline agreed. "People just get wiped out by some hired hit man, and it's never explained."

I shook my head. Somehow that white-haired smiling woman digging up potatoes didn't look the sort to get tangled up in dangerous politics. But then, of course, the woman I saw wasn't Miss Lingworth at all. She was in the pond.

Caroline swung the swivel chair round and carried on Googling. I borrowed the stool from Mum's room and sat next to her, our heads almost touching, her hair feathering my cheek. We could find nothing about Miss Lingworth's personal life until we browsed to an interview in some crusty old journal I'd never heard of; *The Private Lives of Public Figures*. Caroline printed out the page while I sprinted downstairs and made us both some coffee. I was beginning to feel clear-headed now. I even felt excited.

"You OK Shaun?" Mum asked.

"Fine!" I shouted, and raced back upstairs again, anxious to keep up with Caroline. Somewhere in all this information was the clue to her killer. We were on the trail to my acquittal, I felt sure of it.

"'The distinguished political analyst, Winifred Lingworth, speaks to us about her past.'" Caroline read out the article as I set two Simpsons' coffee mugs down on my desk. "'I was born in Liverpool at the end of the Second World War,'" she looked up at me and smiled her thanks, and it felt as if the sun was coming out for me. "'The youngest of two sisters.'"

"Aha! Got her!" I shouted. "This'll be Phyllis."

"Wait on. It then says, 'We couldn't have been less alike. My sister was pretty where I was plain, vivacious where I was a solemn little thing, elegant where I was dumpy, sporty where I had absolutely no co-ordination. I adored her. She mothered me when I was a child. But when it became clear that I was academic and she was not, I went to the grammar school and she to the secondary modern, I to university and she to typing school, the gap between us grew wider and wider. My sister turned against me, she went off to live her own life. Somewhere in Austria, coaching ski-ing. We lost touch with each other.'"

Caroline put the paper down. "There it is then," she said. "The jealous sister. Classic motive."

"Why doesn't she name her though?"

"Because they're estranged. They don't have anything to do with each other."

"Hmm." I read the article again. There was nothing else about the sister. "But they're not alike," I reminded her. "How could I mistake one for the other?"

"Easy. White hair is white hair, and they're both old. Waistlines come and go. It has to be her, Shaun."

"And what's her motive?"

"Revenge. All those years of not being good enough, not being famous or rich or brilliant..."

"...Not even being acknowledged by name... as if she's of no importance at all..."

"...Poor Phyllis couldn't bear it any longer. She came to the cottage to have it out with Win..."

"They fight...."

"No!" Caroline said. "Phyllis poisons her — Win loses consciousness..."

"And Phyllis throws her in the pond to make it look as if she's drowned."

We clapped right hands together, the way tennis doubles players do at Wimbledon. "Phyllis!" we shouted. I felt heady with jubilation. I was cleared!

I slept well that night, the first time for some days. I had almost begun to feel that I was guilty.

8

Next day was Sunday. I fidgeted about all day, finishing off the reconstruction of my bike and cleaning oil off the kitchen floor. The weather turned gloomy; the hills disappeared in grey mist. I could have gone for a quick spin, but I didn't want to leave the house. I was nervous and miserable again. The excitement of last night had fizzled away like a damp firework. I rang Caroline and suggested we should tell the police about Phyllis the sister.

"Hang on," she said. "I don't want to yet. It's still puzzling me. I'm still thinking about it."

She snapped the receiver down. Who did she think she was? Miss Marple? But strangely, I couldn't bring myself to ring the police station either. We didn't want to make fools of ourselves. Mum came back from taking Buster for a walk and told me there was a police car at the top of the track, and policemen all over the place. I didn't want to see it. I didn't ever want to go to that cottage again.

We heard nothing more from the police that day, but even so I took the next morning off school. I just couldn't face the other kids.

"OK," Mum said. "I'll let you have today off, just today. But you must go in tomorrow, Shaun, or there'll be all kinds of rumours flying round. I'm going to work. Ring me if you need me."

I nodded gloomily.

"If they really suspected you, they'd have you in by now," she told me, trying to cheer me up and failing about as miserably as a smiling dentist. "And I've got a very nice solicitor friend I can contact if we need one. He was my boyfriend when I was your age," she sighed. "You should see the size of the house he's got now."

"You married for love," I reminded her.

"And what good did that do me?" She forced a laugh, then gave me a hug, a proper hug as if I was about six years old.

Actually, I don't know, I thought. I've no idea what good it did her. I don't know anything about him. My father is a blank sheet of paper, no face, no name. We simply don't talk about him, ever.

I watched her car drive off and stifled a desire to take my bike to bits again just for something to do. It had started to rain. I doodled round the place, totally bored and wishing now I had gone to school. At least I'd have seen Caroline. And just as I thought about her, telepathic magic, she rang me. The phone was hidden under a pile of washing, and by the time I'd found it and knocked everything on the floor, she'd rung off.

"Oh, Shaun. It's me," the ansaphone said. I rang her back straight away, but there was no reply.

I was so desperate to get in touch with her that I jogged down towards the village, where I could get a signal on my mobile, and texted her instead. *Where r u?* She texted back straight away. *W8 there.* And there she was, coming up the lane, waving at me. I ran to meet her, felt as if I was flying, splashing through puddles, didn't care any more. We were both drenched to the skin. Her hair was stuck round her cheeks; just gorgeous.

"I skipped afternoon school. I'm so worried about you," she said. "I'm sorry about yesterday, when you phoned."

"It's OK. It doesn't matter. I know you're busy."

"I've been ringing people. Things are looking grim. I've got kind of bad news. I've been checking up on the sister. Mum's cousin goes ski-ing in Austria, and I rang her to ask if she could put me in touch with any of the instructors. She's a bit of a flirt. She doesn't just go for the ski-ing, if you know what I mean."

"Aprés-ski." I couldn't take my eyes off her.

"And aprés that. Anyway, she gave me a phone number and I rang this bloke that she met on her last trip — he only speaks German, Shaun, can you imagine? Speaking German on the phone! It was a nightmare. I had to keep putting the phone down so I could look up words in the dictionary. Anyway, I asked him if he knew other ski-ing coaches who live in Austria and he said he could easily find out from various centres, so

61

I said I wanted to contact Phyllis Lingworth. Of course, if she's married she's probably changed her name, so it's a very long shot, and she'll be in her sixties now and so on, but he said he would do what he could. He sounded really nice. I could see why Cousin Belinda fell for him."

I allowed myself a pang of miserable jealousy.

"Great. You're a genius," I said. We were standing outside our house. I fumbled in all my pockets for my house key then realised the door was still open anyway.

"Well, it's not so great. He rang me back about an hour ago. He's been asking around, he said. A retired ski-ing instructor called Miss Lingworth fell from a cable car in Austria a couple of years ago. She broke her spine, she's still very poorly. And her first name, by the way, is Mary."

"Oh God."

"I'm so sorry Shaun."

While she was looking sweetly at me, and I was thinking about holding her hand, the police car drew up outside the house.

9

The slightest bit of rain turns the lane into a river of mud, and we watched, pitiless, the policeman squelching out of the car and scraping his boots as he came up the path. It was the younger one again, the super-fit job who looks as if he spends all his off-duty time in the gym. He scorched a smile at Caroline and I glared at him. Then he asked me if I would mind going back with them to the station for more video questioning.

"No problem," I tried to say, but my mouth was as numb as if I'd had a dentist's injection. I was cold with shock and dread.

"Can I ask why?" Caroline asked bravely, more brave than I was at the time.

"No. Sorry."

Caroline parked herself in front of him. "Can I ask what Miss Lingworth died of?" she demanded. Her face was whiter than I'd ever seen it.

"At this moment in time I am not at liberty to tell you," he said.

I felt helpless, completely without hope. I held my arm out, expecting him to handcuff me.

"Then you'd better take me to the station too," Caroline said. "I saw the woman who was impersonating her. I can identify her. She was called Phyllis."

It didn't help much, but it made me feel a lot better. I gave her a little discreet thumbs up sign, and she did the same to me. He refused to take her in the same car as me though.

"If you want to make a statement, a police-woman will call round later to your house," he told her. He let me ring Mum and she said she would follow me round to the police station straight away. And then he drove me off, without handcuffs, but without giving me a chance to hold Caroline in my arms, which is what I wanted to do, more than anything in the world, to have her arms round me and mine round her and telling each other that everything was going to be all right. Caroline followed us to the gate and stood in the pouring rain, not waving, biting her lip, her hair plastered against her cheeks. I wondered whether I would ever see her again.

At the station they waited for the appropriate adult, Miss Watson, to come. She arrived by taxi, clutching rustling bags of shopping, fresh from the trendy boutiques of Meadow Hall. Meadow Hell, we call it. She smiled at me sorrowfully. Then my old friend Inspector Philip came in and asked me again, and again, to recall the events of my visits to the hidden cottage. I couldn't change my story, there was nothing more to tell. I had a splitting headache. The rain was drumming ceaselessly against the window; the world on the other side was under water, a grey washy blur. If they'd shoved a piece of paper at me and asked me to sign it I think I'd have done so without even reading it, just to be left alone. I wanted to crawl into my bed and sleep till it was all over.

"Why do we have to go through all this again?" I asked.

"Because we are looking for the truth," the Inspector sighed. "Anything. Anything you might have to tell us. How many times did you go to Miss Lingworth's house?"

I couldn't look at him. The truth was, I was scared that I might start blubbing again if I did.

"I went once with Mum. I went twice on my own," I told him.

"When did you first go?"

"Last Monday. The day I found her things."

"Did anyone see you go there?"

"Joe Eldridge. Oh yes, and Jenny."

"Jenny?"

"The post lady. She saw me. She must have told you."

He said nothing.

"She said she saw me."

"Did you see her?"

I stared at him. No. I hadn't even thought about that before. If Jenny had seen me, why hadn't I seen her? Where had her van been? Surely I'd have seen a bright red post office van in that little lane. I shook my head. My heart was bumping in my ribs. "I didn't see her. I didn't see her post van. But she said she saw me, Inspector. So where was she?"

At last they let me go home. Mum was waiting for me outside. Just as we were leaving, the farmer neighbour, Joe Eldridge, arrived in a police car and clambered out, shaking himself as if he had the dust of his fields in his clothes. We glared at each other, but Mum touched my elbow and guided me away from him to the car.

"He looks guilty," I muttered.

"He looks worried, that's for sure. I heard at the medical centre that his wife's telling everyone she saw him going to Miss Lingworth's cottage," Mum whispered.

"So she's given him up to the police. Good for her!" I twisted round to look at him.

"Innocent till proved guilty," Mum reminded me.

"What must it be like to live with someone like him?" I asked.

"Well, she doesn't, not any more. They're saying she's left the farm and gone to live with Molly Oldroyd."

"Why Molly?"

"Molly's her grandmother, apparently. No, I didn't know either. It seems that everybody is related to everybody else in this village. You have to be careful what you say. Molly's family is spread out all over Edale, cousins and so on, related from way back. There's a couple of other families like that. They own most of Edale between them. They compete with each other to buy everyone out. You know what they say round here? 'When there's a death, boundaries walk.'"

"What on earth's that supposed to mean?"

"Think about it." Mum started the car up. The windscreen wipers came on, ticking away like my brain doing its calculations. I was feeling better already. There was obviously some connection, if only I could figure it out.

"I heard Molly telling you on the phone that she'd written to Win Lingworth about the cottage. Maybe she wanted to buy it."

"Oh yes, she'd love that." Mum laughed. "There's such a lot of land with it, bordering on to the farm."

"So she owns the farm behind Win Lingworth's?"

"Well, her grand-daughter married into that one. Joe's family have farmed there for years, and now Rhoda is married to him, it will be hers too."

All this was potentially interesting. I tucked it away in my fizzing brain for future reference, and drifted into a fidgety doze while Mum drove me home.

"I didn't like him," I said, hours later, it seemed, when we were nearly at our house. We had just passed the end of the track that led to Miss Lingworth's cottage and Eldridge's Farm. Rainwater gushed round the wheelie bins. "Mum, I bet he did it."

Mum shook her head. "Don't say that. Joe's all right. But he's got a temper on him these days, I'm told. Doing a lot of shouting, though it's usually at his old sheepdog. I wouldn't like to get on the wrong side of him on a dark night. Or his wife, for that matter. She's got a tongue like a bread knife." We swished on down to our lane. "Don't get me wrong," she added. "They're all lovely people." She can do a really good demolition job, Mum can, and then she'll always repent. "Especially Molly. She's a sweetie really. Crazy about bird watching. It's no wonder she sees everything that's going on. She's always looking through binoculars! I'm really very fond of her."

Molly, I thought. Some sweetie. If she's Joe's mother-in-law then they must be all in this together. Don't be fooled Mum, I thought.

Not long after we came home, Leslie breezed in, his spectacles glittering with good cheer. He usually wears civvies in the daytime, but he was here on business today, dog collar and all.

"Fancy knocking a ball round the tennis court later, Shaun?" he said. "The rain's stopped, and it's going to be a lovely evening." That was his way of offering pastoral support, but it was the last thing I wanted. He always beats me anyway. I just kept my head down while he and Mum chewed the cud over what they knew about Miss Lingworth; poor Miss Lingworth, as she was now referred to.

"I only visited her once," Leslie said, easing his collar with his little finger. I always felt that he should cut a hole in it for his Adam's apple. I suggested it once.

"I went up to bless her cottage when she moved in. She made it quite clear that I wasn't welcome. 'I don't like visitors,' she said, 'of any sort.' Polite enough, friendly, but I took the hint. Never went again. You have to respect people's wishes for privacy, if that's what they want. I wanted to ask her if she'd like to join the Horticultural Society — she obviously loves gardening. She's let it go recently though. Shame."

He stood up, swiping an imaginary top-spin across the table at me. "Let me know if you change your mind, Shaun."

"Here," Mum said. "perhaps you'd like to take this with you." And she gave him the bottle of strawberry wine, scooping it off the table as if she was saving it from any imaginary return I might make. He dropped his pretend racquet at once.

"How kind of you!" he said. "How did you know it was my favourite?"

"I didn't," Mum said. "Miss Lingworth, well, whoever it was who was impersonating Miss Lingworth, gave it to Shaun. She made it."

"She made it?" He turned the bottle round and held it up to the light. "It looks very like Gregoria's. I could have sworn it's her bottle, her label, her wonderful strawberry wine. Nobody makes wine quite like Gregoria. Are you sure you don't want it?"

"I couldn't bear to drink it now," Mum said. "I can't bear to look at it, knowing what happened to poor Win Lingworth."

"The police might need it," I said. It was *my* present, after all.

"If they did need it they'd have taken it by now. Anyway, we can tell them where it's gone. I just don't want it in the house."

"I'll put it on the bottle tombola at the church fair," the vicar promised. "Nobody need know its macabre connections. And it does look rather delicious. Gregoria will be quite put out when she sees it."

"Who's Gregoria?" I asked.

"Oh, you must know Gregoria. She lives by the mill. She always wins the home-made wine prize at the village show."

Something about that was important too, though I couldn't quite put the pieces together. I made a mental note to tell Caroline about it. She arrived just as Mum was giving Leslie the wine bottle, and she just slipped past him and ran up to my room, waving her notebook at me. She would be Googling away on my computer again. One good thing had come out of all this; she was at my house a lot now. It had become natural to have her around, as if she was one of the family. It was always like that when we were kids, even when Mum and I lived in Sheffield. Our mums had known each other since their student days. Either her mum was minding me or mine was minding Caroline, especially when we first moved to Edale and didn't know anyone else. But by that time I was ten and girls were to be avoided as much as possible. Then Caroline got girly and spent most of her time at the riding stables. And then, our first day at the new school, I looked at her on the bus and thought, she's beautiful, and I haven't really stopped thinking about that since.

Yet we still hadn't kissed, hadn't even held hands. How do you hold hands with someone you used to scrap with like a sister? There was a whole new set of rules to be learnt now.

I pounded up the stairs as soon as Leslie had gone. Caroline had her back to me, flicking from page to page on the computer. Her hair glowed. I wanted to touch it. I put out my hand, so lightly that she would never feel it. It hovered there, just above her head.

"They've taken Joe Eldridge in for questioning," I said. "You know, the farmer who lives behind Miss Lingworth."

"They've got to question him," she said, "But he didn't do it, any more than you did."

"How do you know?" I asked.

She swung round to look at me and I lifted my hand away quickly. "Why on earth would he? No, I think we've got to find out who that woman is."

"That Phyllis person. Can you find that article again?"

"I already have. I showed it to a policewoman this morning. They know all about her anyway. They've contacted her apparently, to identify the body. Doesn't it sound horrible, Shaun? Poor Miss Lingworth. Anyway, she's Phyllis Jordan.

She's actually her literary agent."

"Oh wow! Well that's it then! Greedy agent wants more than her ten per cent." I was getting fired up. "Knocks her on the head, shoves her in the pond, and makes off with the sock under the mattress which is full of Win's prize money."

"Except," said Caroline, "She didn't win prize money, she won a medal. Just a big honour thing. She even got an OBE for her research, apparently. And anyway, look at the photograph. There's the names underneath. The agent is the one on the right."

I scanned the photograph. "Oh," I said, completely deflated. Phyllis Jordan was black.

"You got it," said Caroline.

Yet I still felt strange, looking along the row of faces. I felt irrationally cold and slightly sick with trembling. One by one, as I read the caption, I put names to faces. "His Excellency, the Head of State —, Governor this —, Phyllis Jordan, Baroness that, Vice-Consul, what a load of bigwigs. Who's this one on the end though? There's no name."

"That's the one I'm searching for now. Here she is."

She clicked the mouse, and brought the article up on screen. She zoomed in on the photograph, clicking to the end of the row, enlarging the unnamed woman's face with its full, beaming smile, the eyes bright in the flash of the camera. Short dark hair, but not young. For some reason I was shaking again.

"Let's think again about when you went to the cottage. I still wonder if that wine is significant." Caroline said. "Don't you think it was strange, giving a sixteen-year-old boy a bottle of home-made wine, of all things?" She suddenly pushed back her chair. "I'm going crazy, sitting here. I'm going home for a bit. See you later." And she ran lightly down the stairs and was out of the house before I had the chance to say thank you. And I hadn't put my hand on her hair, her beautiful brown glossy hair.

10

I was as fidgety as a hamster in a cage by then. I had to get out. I fished my super-clean bike out of the shed and decided to go for a spin. The hills and fields were washed bright and brilliant, and the sky was heading up for a golden September sunset. It felt better to be out of the house. It felt great, till I approached the green wheelie bins. In the distance I could hear Joe Eldridge on his quad, rounding up his sheep, yelling at them to behave, cursing his dog. So the police hadn't kept him in. Anyway, I had no intention of going down that lane and being treated to one of his friendly greetings, but as I cycled past the bins I couldn't help glancing down it. Now I could hear someone whistling. A purple hand shot up from behind a bush, waving at me.

"No," I told myself. "Don't go down that road, Shaun Parker. Ignore the purple hand."

I put my head down and belted towards the village. Someone beeped a horn at me, and I nearly went into the tender arms of the hawthorn hedge again. I looked up to see Tom Hemsley grinning away at the wheel of his dad's car. As he passed me he wound down the window and shouted did I need a lift.

"Wally!" I shouted back. "Road hog!"

He was heading down the village road in the direction of Caroline's house. I straddled my bike and watched as he pulled up right outside her door. At that moment all the bright, positive evening dissolved for me. So that was why Caroline had left my house so abruptly. She had a date with the best looking boy in our school. And he had a car. A British Racing Green Rover, to be exact. He would take her to Ladybower or over to Castleton. He'd drive her up Winnat's Pass and they'd watch the sunset from Mam Tor. I couldn't bear the thought of it.

I did a U-turn round the vicar, who was just crossing the road, super-fit in his immaculate whites, to go to the tennis court. He's always there, and he'll challenge anyone in the valley to a game. When he fits his God stuff in I don't know.

"Everything OK, Shaun?" he called.

"Fine thanks, Leslie," I lied.

And then I pulled up sharply, remembering his conversation with Mum. There was definitely something there that didn't quite ring true. I nodded curtly at him and cycled off down the valley road. If he'd only been to Win Lingworth's house once, *how did he know she'd let her garden grow wild*? Hmm? I tucked the question away in a filing drawer in my head marked 'suspicious'. I'll go and consult Caroline about it, I thought, and then I remembered her treachery and decided against it.

I'd no idea where I was going then. Partly because I didn't want to see Tom's car speeding past me with Caroline smiling and waving from the passenger seat, and partly because I'd just had a stroke of pure intuitive genius about one of my other suspects, I screeched to a halt outside Molly Oldroyd's and trundled my bike up the path to her front door.

She didn't hear me knocking, but the door's always open. She was sitting at the table, concentrating on placing a roof piece of a three-dimensional jigsaw puzzle. I gave her such a start when I walked in that her hand knocked against it and the whole Buckingham Palace of a structure collapsed.

"Blast!" she said cheerfully. "Hello Shaun! Why don't you just walk right in?"

"I'm sorry Molly. I did knock."

I heard someone coming down the creaking stairs, pause, then scuttle up again.

"You got mice," I laughed.

"That was Rhoda," Molly said. "My granddaughter. She's a bag of nerves at the moment. Well, not surprising, is it? Her nearest neighbour is murdered and the culprit's still on the loose. It's very distressing."

"Any idea who might have done it?" I asked, as casual as a cat. I was strolling round the room as I was talking, scanning the neat piles of jigsaw puzzles, bird books and sheets of music that were heaped up on every surface. By the door was a racquet and a bag of tennis balls, a pair of brown gleaming walking boots, a pile of parish magazines, but not the thing I was looking for.

"I'm thinking about it," Molly said. "What a mystery it all is! It's certainly given the village something to talk about. Who murdered poor Miss Lingworth? Poor Miss Lingworth my foot!" Her voice was suddenly tight with scorn. "What did she contribute to the village? Nothing! Wouldn't even do me an article for the *Ringing Roger*, and she was a writer! Hardly ever clapped eyes on the woman, and how many years had she lived there? Long before you and your mother moved to the valley. She hardly set foot in the village, and she hardly set foot out of it. I know. I notice these things. Nobody visited her. What was she up to, eh?"

She scooped up some of the jigsaw pieces and started again on the balancing act of slotting them into place. I don't know how she can do it and talk at the same time, but she's probably well practised in both. "I've been keeping my eye on that old cottage for some time. Very few comings and goings — I think she just lived off her vegetable patch, or used to, till she let it go wild. She had some furniture delivered there about a year ago — I don't know how they managed to get the van down that bumpy track. I was worried that she might have sold the old place behind my back, so I kept a watch. But no, no newcomers, thank goodness. Don't want any more strangers here, London types. No, it's all a big mystery." She rubbed her hands together gleefully and darted me a nut-brown, twinkling glance. "I love mysteries. Oh, poor Win Lingworth."

"I think you should tell the police," I said, "You know, that you've been keeping a watch on the place. Mind if I get a drink of water?" I wandered into the kitchen. And found what I was looking for, perched on the windowsill next to some pots of sprawling herbs.

"Molly," I called. "When you told me you'd lost something, was it these?"

I walked back in, dangling a pair of binoculars on their strap. They were identical to the ones I'd seen on Miss Lingworth's gate. The strap, for a start, was a piece of orange twine that farmers use on bags of feed.

"Yes, it was! Aren't I foolish! I've been up and down the valley looking for them, couldn't think where I'd left them."

"So they were on your kitchen windowsill all the time?" I heard a tread on the stair. The granddaughter was standing there, listening, hiding. It made my flesh creep, knowing I was being spied on.

"Heavens, no. Joe found them somewhere. He brought them here when he was dropping some of Rhoda's clothes off. He didn't come in, just dumped them on the doorstep. He's like that these days. He's got a grudge on his shoulders the size of the church steeple. So I still don't know where he picked the binoculars up. Another of life's mysteries!"

"I think you should tell the police about that, too. And if you don't, then I will."

I left her and the spy on the stairs to muse over that. Feeling pleasantly smug, I cycled home and ate the biggest meal I'd had for days. I even told Mum I'd wash up while she took Buster for a walk.

"She's found a new walk, you know," Mum said, collecting her things while Buster hurled herself against the door to be let out. "But it's a bit muddy, so I need my boots for it. There must be a lot of rabbits that way. Up past the derelict barn."

"Oh yes. She dragged me that way last week," I called back. "It joins up with an old bridle path. Be careful — I nearly got run down by a mountain bike."

"Do you know," said Mum. "If you carry on down that bridle path, I think it ends up round the back of Miss Lingworth's cottage. See you later!"

I stood with the tea towel in my hand, staring after her and Buster, and it all came back to me. Buster had taken me up that overgrown track last week. It goes across a muddy field full of rusty farm equipment, past a derelict barn, and then plunges down to a stream. Buster splashed through, I followed, jumping from stone to stone, then scrambled up a bank and found myself on a stony track running down from the hill. I went down it, wondering if it would bring me back onto the lane. I smelt wood smoke, and dimly realised that I must be near a house, though I couldn't see it. I could hear a woman's voice raised, calling someone or shouting about something. I saw a farmer striding across a field, and then heard a *crack!* as he shot a rabbit. A cyclist whizzed down from behind me, splattering me with mud. An ecstatic Buster gave chase. But I didn't go any further. I called Buster back, worried about the farmer and his shotgun, put her lead on and dragged her home. She hated me for it. But that was well over a week ago. I remember well, Thursday night, Mum's Pilates night, a whole ten days ago. The night Win Lingworth was murdered.

The Inspector was right. I was there.

Maybe I should ring him now. Or was it better to just leave it there. I'd told him so many times that I'd only been to the cottage three times; what would he think if I came up with it now — "Oh, by the way, I've just remembered...."

I decided to leave it. He seemed to believe me last time. If he asked me again, I'd tell him.

Or would it be worse, much worse, to leave it till then? Witholding information. Wasting police time. Obstructing the police in the course of their enquiries. Perverting the course of justice — a whole catalogue of crimes. I was sweating by now.

I desperately wanted to ask Caroline's advice. I picked up the phone, and then remembered Tom grinning at me from his father's car, and I put the receiver down again. I plunged my hands into the washing up bowl and clattered through the pans, splashing sudsy water over everywhere. I was in a fury with myself. I hated myself that night.

The phone was staring at me the whole time, demanding to be used, and in the end I gave in. Nothing is worse than suspecting something and not being sure. It was better to know the truth. I dialled Caroline's number. I felt sick. I almost put the receiver down again when I heard her voice.

"Caroline," I said. I could feel my voice shaking, and pretended to clear my throat a couple of times. "Where've you been?"

"Where?" she repeated.

"Did you enjoy the ride?"

"What ride?"

I swallowed. She wasn't making it easy. "In Tom's car."

"Well, I'd love a ride in Tom's car," she said. "But he hasn't invited me."

"He went to your house," I said stubbornly. Mum always says, when I dig a hole, I'm trying to get to Australia.

"Did he? Oh, he probably went next door to see Matthew. Why would he come to see me? What's all this about?" She paused. I cringed like a cat. I could almost see her smiling. I could hear the dancing in her voice. "Shaun?"

This was awful. Fool, fool, I said to myself. I wished I'd never started it. I felt so stupid. Stop torturing yourself, Mum would have said. Out with it! Spit it out.

"So where were you?" I asked lamely.

"You know very well where I was! I waved to you."

My mind reeled back to the bike ride. I'd seen Tom. I'd seen Leslie on his way to the tennis court. I'd nearly seen Joe Eldridge at the blunt end of his bellowing voice.

"Where?" I asked.

"I was helping Gregoria to pick blackberries. By the green wheelie bins."

I grinned and ambled out into the garden with the phone. "Caroline of the purple hand?" I suddenly felt rapturous. If I *was* a cat I'd have been purring.

"Yes, very. I saw Gregoria by Win Lingworth's lane — well, at least, I heard her whistling — and decided to check her out, just in case she knew anything about the strawberry wine. Well, she's famous for it round here, so I wanted to know what she thought about her rival wine-maker. I keep seeing her there — she's been up and down that lane all week picking blackberries for her winemaking. Apparently Joe snarls at her every time he sees her in case she trespasses through his gate, so she hides behind the brambles when she hears him coming. I do like Gregoria. She's so funny. She eats as many blackberries as she picks."

"Purple mouth," I said.

"I'll say. She looks like a were-wolf when she's

finished! Anyway, I wanted to check her out because I know she's one of your suspects. Just as I was leaving, I asked her whether she ever makes any strawberry wine."

"And does she?"

"She went a bit strange, I must say. She kind of stiffened and wanted to know why I was asking about it, and then muttered something about having to be extremely careful what you drink! I've no idea what she meant. And she wouldn't say anything else, just went tight-lipped."

"Purple-lipped."

"You could say."

"Hmm. Doesn't look too good, however nice she is. The police should be questioning her."

"They already have."

"Aha. Well, I've been checking up on Molly."

"Good thinking."

I could feel myself glowing. I plucked one of Mum's last yellow roses and sniffed it. I would give it to Caroline. "Did you know Rhoda Eldridge is her grand-daughter? Oh, you do. Well, anyway, she was behaving very suspiciously, snooping on the stairs while I was talking to Molly. She's left Joe, by the way. Oh. You know everything. But listen, those binoculars I saw on the gate belong to Molly! What do you make of that? Why were they on Win Lingworth's gate? But even stranger, it was Joe who found them there. What was he doing there?"

I shook the rose so the last glistening drops of rain oozed out of it. She wouldn't mind, would she, if I gave her a rose? Or would she think I was pathetic?

"What else did you find out?" she asked.

"Molly doesn't like Win Lingworth. Didn't. She's been spying on her, by all accounts. That's probably why the binocs. were there. They're good at spying, that family. And, by the way, did you know this? 'When there's a death, boundaries walk'."

I sensed that I had lost Caroline's attention. I could hear her with someone at the other end of the phone. "Shaun, I've got to go," she said. "Mum wants the phone. We'll have a think about these things and talk about them."

"Later," I said.

"Tomorrow."

I was feeling elated when I went back into the house. I put the rose in a jam jar for tomorrow, and picked up the copy of the newspaper photograph of Win Lingworth's award ceremony. As soon as I looked at it I got that cold, clammy feeling all over again, reminding me that this was no game. Win Lingworth had been murdered. I looked again at all the people on the photograph, and stopped at the dark-haired smiling woman at the end of the row. Those bright, intelligent eyes stared back at me, right into me.

"It's her," I whispered.

11

I still had the photograph in my hand an hour later. I was very clever. I'd found some felt pens and whitened her hair, filled up the background in black to shorten it. Then I drew glasses on her face. Such a simple disguise, so easy. And then you only had to look from the woman in the centre of the photograph to the woman at the end of the row to see how alike they were. The only marked difference between them was that one was smiling and the other one wasn't. But I still couldn't make any sense out if anything.

I went to get some food from the kitchen, and realised that Mum was still out with Buster. She'd been away much too long; it was growing dark. She ought to have been back by now. I began to feel nervous about her. She was mad, staying out on her own at this time of night. Maybe I ought to go looking for her. Where on earth was she? I paced round the house, peering out of the windows at the disappearing lane and the shadowy trees reaching up to the black hills. *Come back Mum, come back Mum*, I kept muttering. There's a murderer on the loose. Didn't she have any sense? I couldn't read, couldn't face telly, or homework, or anything.

I must have dropped off to sleep on top of my bed, still clutching the paper printout, because I was suddenly jerked awake when I was aware of a stealthy rustling sound outside in the garden. I lay with my eyes wide open, listening to it. Next minute something scratched against my window. I nearly shouted out loud. There it came again. I slid off the bed and dropped to my knees. A flickering light flashed into the room, and away again. And then again, that scratching sound like fingernails on the glass. On my hands and knees I crept to the window, keeping my head down. My heart was pounding. My ears were straining to every sound. I heard someone hissing my name.

I sat just under the window with my head in my hands for a bit, not knowing what on earth to do. The scratching came again, just above my head, but I couldn't see what was causing it. In the end I couldn't stand it any longer. I knelt up and turned myself round, and risked a glance over the sill. A dark figure stood on the lawn, holding a long branch in both hands. I pushed up the window.

"Caroline! What d'you think you're doing!"

"Ssh!" she whispered. "I don't want your mum to hear."

"She's out!" I whispered back. I clattered down the stairs and opened the door.

"Listen," she said, "Don't fuss, just get your shoes and come with me."

"Where to?" I was digging my feet into my trainers as I spoke.

"Win Lingworth's."

"What! You're mad! It's nearly dark!"

"That's why I'm going now. We absolutely have to, Shaun."

And she was off, jogging down the path and out into the lane, her dark hair bouncing, and like a mad fool I followed her.

Miss Lingworth's, of all places. In the dark, of all times. Nothing in the world could look more suspicious.

We ducked under the 'scene of crime tape' that was stretched across the gate, and Caroline loped round to the back garden. She shone her torch all round it.

"Just as I thought."

"What?"

"Tell you later. Let's get in the house."

"Caroline," I protested. "This is going to look really bad, if we're caught."

"Things couldn't look worse for you than they do already," she said calmly.

"Then why are we doing it?"

"Looking for clues."

Both the front door and the back were locked now. She picked up a stone, smashed the kitchen window, and carefully stretched in her hand to lift up the catch. She opened the window fully.

"Do you want to go in first?"

"Caroline," I said. "This is mad."

"Or you can wait outside if you want to," she said.

"But we shouldn't be doing this at all."

"Or you can go to prison for the rest of your life. Take your pick."

So I went in head first, and opened the door for Caroline.

"Look in the cellar and the kitchen," she hissed.

"What for?"

"Anything. Wine. And stuff to make it with. I'm going upstairs. Oh, don't put the light on. Here, I've brought you another torch." She paused for a minute, flashing the torch round the kitchen, then trailing the beam across the floor.

"Mm," she said thoughtfully.

"What?"

She crouched down and put her hand under the table. "Tell you later. Take the torch." And she ran lightly up the stairs.

I groped round the kitchen, flashing the little torch whenever I dared. The cupboards were empty; no food except a jar of instant coffee and a box of teabags. Fridge empty. I felt terrible doing this, prowling round the house of a dead woman, a murdered woman. I was shaking so badly that I knocked a wine glass off the draining board. Just in time I jammed my hip against the cupboard and stopped it from smashing on the floor. I found the door to the cellar and opened it cautiously. This was worse, much worse, than anything I'd ever done in my life.

The cellar was tidy and clean, but virtually empty. It had the usual damp, mushroomy smell of cellars, but something else as well, a sharpish, rusty sort of smell that I couldn't identify. I could almost taste it. It was a very narrow space, and had such a low ceiling that I had to duck my head to work my way through it. I swept my torch round it, lighting up a vacuum cleaner that was bent over like a skinny little old man, but nothing else except the dark stain of a damp patch on the floor. Certainly no bottles or demijohns or any of that paraphernalia that wine-makers use. I'd helped my granddad sometimes, when we lived with him in Sheffield, so I knew what to look for. Then I heard a sound from above me, a click of a key being turned in a lock. I tried to get my bearings. Surely it was the front door.

Someone was unlocking the front door.

I backed quickly towards the cellar door — I couldn't turn round because the cellar was so narrow at this point. But from behind me I heard, very gently, the cellar door closing. I could hardly breathe now. I was still hunched over with my shoulders pressed to the ceiling and my back to the door. And I knew, I absolutely knew, that someone had come into the cellar and was standing right behind me. I was too scared to turn round, too scared to speak.

"Switch the torch off," the someone whispered.

Shaking, I did as I was told.

It was pitch dark, and I was trapped in a tiny cellar with a murderer. I thought I might pass out at any minute. I heard myself groaning.

A hand touched my shoulder, a voice hissed. "Ssh! There's someone in the house!"

Only then did I realise that it was Caroline in the cellar with me. I shuffled myself round and groped out for her. I gripped her arm. She put her face close to my ear.

"Someone came in through the front door."

"I heard them," I said. "Who is it?"

"No idea. I heard them coming up the path and I ran down to warn you."

"What shall we do?"

"Nothing."

So we stood in the darkness doing nothing, her face so close to mine that I could feel her breath on my cheek, and it felt as if the darkness was alive with electricity.

We heard someone going upstairs and moving about up there. No voices, so it was only one person. We heard the sound of a drawer being pulled open and pushed back in again, then another. The footsteps moved away into another room, and we lost the sounds, however hard we strained to listen.

"Shall we run for it?" I whispered.

"No," Caroline whispered back. "Wait."

Just as well she said that, because immediately we heard the footsteps coming down the stairs, fast this time, clattering above our heads, then out through the front door. The door was pulled shut, a key turned in the lock, and then the footsteps died away down the path. For what seemed like an eternity we stood listening. At last we relaxed. I realised then that I'd been gripping Caroline's arm all this time.

"You all right?" I asked softly.

"Fine," she said. "Let's get out of here."

We didn't dare switch on our torches. We crept up the cellar steps and fumbled our way to the kitchen. I was just groping my way towards the door when a dark figure appeared in the doorway, framed in the moonlight.

It was the ghost of Win Lingworth.

12

"How dare you trespass in my house!" She stepped forward and closed the door behind her. We could hardly see her now, just the pale gleam of her hair.

Caroline and I stood motionless. Neither of us spoke. We couldn't think of a thing to say.

"I should phone the police straight away. I should tell them you've been trespassing. I'm sure they'll be very interested."

I dug my hands in my pockets. This was deep, deep trouble. This was the nightmare come true.

"But I'm prepared to overlook it, if you tell me what you were doing here."

"We haven't taken anything," I said. "We were just — looking round."

"*Looking round*!" The woman's voice was heavy with scorn. "You break into a house where a criminal investigation is under way, just to *look round*! Have you any idea how serious this is?"

"We were looking for clues," Caroline said. "The police have been questioning Shaun for days, but we just wanted to see if we could find anything that might, I don't know, help them with their enquiries. We want to find out who did it."

How lame it sounded. What a pair of kids we must have seemed.

"I'm still waiting for a proper answer."

There was a long silence. I was waiting for Caroline to speak, but she said nothing. Shapes were blooming now we were getting used to the darkness. I could make out the woman's face, the table, the broken window, Caroline.

"Don't be stupid," The woman snapped. "I'm saving you from getting into serious trouble. Just tell me why you were trepassing in my house, and we'll say no more about it."

"We're not trespassing in your house," Caroline said at last. "This is Miss Lingworth's cottage, and she's dead. If anyone's trespassing here, it's you. Would you mind telling us who you are?"

"How dare you! Impudent as well as foolish. But seeing that you are being so pedantic, you should know that I am Mary Lingworth, and that I have recently inherited the cottage from my dear sister, Winifred."

"I see," said Caroline. She looked sideways at me, as if to prompt me to say something. But I didn't see at all. None of this made any sense to me.

"We thought Mary Lingworth was very ill in hospital. Somewhere in Austria."

"Graz," Caroline added.

I could hear a smile in the woman's voice. "My word, you've been doing your homework. But not thoroughly enough. I am, as you see, fully recovered, and have come to take over my sister's estate. I am her only living relative, and I have inherited everything. Including what you have probably stolen." She fished in her pocket and brought out a mobile phone. It was a large, black old-fashioned one. I have only ever seen one as big and clumsy as that in my life. It was the one I had found in the jacket pocket on the track to the hidden cottage. Even so, it was no use here. "So, am I to phone the police, or are you going to return my sister's belongings to me?"

I frowned. Could she be talking about the things she'd lost in the lane? Or something else?

"There was a purse, a jacket, a pair of binoculars, and a mobile phone. That mobile phone," I said, pointing to the one in her hand, lit by a cast of moonlight as if it was a prop in a stage play. "Nothing else."

In the growing light of the kitchen I could just see the half smile that flickered across her face. Surely it *was* her; the woman in the garden, beaming at me because her silly trick had worked. I was sure it was her. So the woman I had met that day was actually the sister? But surely that was before the body had been discovered.

"I've no idea what you're talking about," she said.

"When you gave me the bottle of wine."

"Wine?"

Had I imagined the woman in the garden? I felt I was going mad. The last few days were dissolving away from me, there was no sequence to any of the events any more. Was I really talking to Mary Lingworth, or to a ghost, the ghost of Win Lingworth?

"Something that was my sister's is missing," she insisted.

"We've taken nothing," I repeated. "Why don't you ask the police? They've probably taken it to forensics." I was trying to be helpful. It must be awful, I thought, to know that your sister had been murdered, even if you had been estranged from her for years. I wished we had never broken into the place like that. I wanted to wind everything back so that we were no longer in the cottage, had never even thought of going there. The air was so heavy with mixed messages and memories, it was impossible to think clearly. I just wanted to get out, to get out and go home and forget the cottage ever existed.

"Can we go?" Caroline asked, reading my mood. "We're very sorry we intruded. And we're sorry we can't help you, but perhaps you could let us go home now."

Mary Lingworth passed a hand over her face in a gesture of utter weariness. "You may as well. I'm sure you can imagine, it's been a very difficult time for me. I want to do my best you know, for my sister. I want to keep everything intact, everything as it used to be." Her voice trembled slightly. "Yes. Please. Go."

She opened the door quickly, banishing us into the night, and shut and bolted it again as soon as we were outside.

13

Fresh air had never smelt so sweet, stars had never looked so bright. Still we kept to the shadows as we crept towards the gate and into the track. I grabbed Caroline's hand and we ran until we were onto the valley lane. A car swept past us, bringing the real world of ordinary people back into our lives.

"I thought she was a ghost at first,"I panted. "Didn't you?"

Caroline nodded, wide-eyed, her breath bursting out of her.

"Do you want me to see you home?" I asked.

"Yours is nearer. I just want to get away from here."

"Right," I said. My head was spinning.

We set off again, running towards my house, our gasping breath bumping up and down in time with our feet. All we wanted was to get away from the hidden cottage and the shadows and the memory of the stifling mushroomy rusty air in the cellar, the footsteps on the creaking stairs, the ghostly figure in the doorway. We flung ourselves into my house and into the bright sanctuary of the kitchen and sank down, heaving for breath.

And then I stood up so suddenly that my chair

screamed on the tiles.

"What's up?" Caroline gasped.

"No Buster." I ran into the living room. "Mum?" I shouted. "Mum?" I ran upstairs and looked in the bathroom, her bedroom, my bedroom, and back down again.

"Something's happened to Mum, Caroline."

"Calm down. What d'you mean?"

"She went out just after six o'clock to take Buster for a walk. She's usually half an hour, an hour at the most. What time is it now? Half ten. She's been gone over four hours!"

"Perhaps she went up on Rushup Edge."

"In the dark?"

"It's a lovely starry night. Lovely night for a walk, really. We'll give her half an hour, shall we, and if she hasn't turned up then I'll phone Dad and ask him to bring the car over. You're just getting jittery, after what happened."

I tried to relax. Caroline put the kettle on and I got some chocolate digestives out of the cupboard. They're the only biscuits that count. Has to be dark chocolate though.

"Can you believe it?" I asked. "Mary Lingworth, of all people. We weren't imagining it, were we?"

"No. We weren't imagining it."

"I thought it was Win Lingworth."

"It did look like her."

"But it could have been anyone, really. We didn't really see her face clearly. And I don't know what Win Lingworth looked like any more. Anyway, she scared me out of my wits, the way she stepped into the kitchen like that. I really thought she was a ghost!"

Caroline started giggling. I put a tea towel over my head and lunged round the kitchen making *whoo*ing sounds. We were both howling with hysteria till we were weak with laughter. It made us feel better. It chased away the ghost, anyway.

"So, what did we find out?" I asked when we'd calmed down. There were bits of crumb on Caroline's lip. I wanted to wipe them off. Better, lick them off. "There was no sign of wine-making kit."

She brushed the crumbs away. "No sign of old strawberry plants in the garden, either."

"So she didn't make that wine herself."

"Probably not."

"You found something on the kitchen floor," I reminded her.

"Yes, I saw it shining. Just a tiny splinter of glass in the crack of one of the tiles. And there was a big patch on the kitchen floor as if there'd been a rug down there once."

"That was the funny smell in the cellar! Damp carpet sort of smell. There wasn't anything down there though, except an old vacuum cleaner. So that was all."

"Not quite. I found these in the bedroom." Caroline pulled some photos out of her pocket and laid them on the table.

"Caroline!" I was utterly shocked. "So you did take something! Why didn't you give them to her?"

"Because I wanted a chance to look at them, that's why," she said simply.

She spread them out on the table and laid them out in some sort of order. Seven photos in all, some black and white, some in colour. We stood together, serious now, looking at them all carefully. Two smiling little girls in party clothes, one fair, one dark. The same two a bit older, schoolgirls, the dark-haired one wearing glasses. Two graduates in cap and gown, both dark-haired, both wearing glasses. The same two, older, young women at a conference of some sort. Another of the same pair, middle-aged women on a walking holiday, noticeably greying. And the photograph we had seen on the Internet.

"They're not the same pair, are they?" I said. "This fair-haired one in these early photographs must be the sister?"

"Win and Mary. And these older ones — definitely Win. But who's with her? A friend?" She flicked one of them over. *With Alison Crow* was written in neat handwriting on the back.

"So." She picked them up again and spread them out like a hand of cards, frowning at them. "Alison Crow."

"What are you thinking?" I asked.

"Nothing. My brain's hurting too much to think." She shuffled them again and then stacked them together.

"We'll have to take them back," I said.

"Mmm. But not now."

"No. Not now. I'm not going down her lane again tonight. But she might still report us to the police."

"We'll have to take a chance on that."

"She must be telling the truth," I decided. "About being Mary. She was completely blank about the bottle of wine. So that was a different woman that I saw that day at the cottage. Had to be, because the dates don't fit. Anyway, maybe the bottle isn't important."

"It could be. It could be the murder weapon."

"Uh-uh," I shook my head. "The vicar's got it, intact, remember."

Caroline shrugged. "Maybe there were two bottles. Remember she told you that was her last bottle"

"OK. And — ?"

"The murderer hit Win on the head with it?"

"Which would explain the splinter of glass. Not quite cleaned up."

"And the missing rug. Got wet with wine..."

"And blood..."

"Shoved it down the cellar out of the way."

"Where's the rug now though?"

"Police took it for examination." Caroline twisted her hair round her fingers. "Or maybe the murderer didn't hit her with it. Maybe she was poisoned, like we first thought."

I had a chocolate digestive biscuit half way in my mouth. I drew it out again. "Poisoned her with wine?"

"Mmm. Let's go through this. Say the murderer poisoned Miss Lingworth, but had brought two bottles just in case — well, in case the poison didn't work the first time."

"OK." I nodded slowly. "The first bottle works."

"The first one works. Win slumps on floor, breaking her glass, spilling the last dregs as she goes. Then the murderer dumps Win in the pond, washes the bottle out and puts it in the wheelie bin down the lane."

"The bin men take it away."

"But she's still got the other one. She has to get rid of it."

"She?"

"I think it's got to be the women you met."

"OK." Privately I arranged my suspects in my head. I decided to keep them there for the time being.

"So she gives it to you."

I stared at her. My heart was doing slow somersaults again. "She gives it to me. She tells me to drink it all by myself."

"She wanted to poison you," Caroline said flatly.

"Why?"

"Because you'd seen her. You're probably the only one who saw her there, pretending to be Win Lingworth."

"But she led me there deliberately," I reminded her. "She wanted me to see her."

"There'll be a reason. Ah, wait. She wanted

you to be found with a bottle of poisoned wine! So, the plot is, sixteen year old boy poisons lonely writer, then poisons himself."

"I feel sick," I said. I ate another biscuit.

"So do I. But it didn't work, did it?" The ghost of her beautiful smile drifted across her face and away again. "Anyway, the real question is, why did she do it?"

"And who is she?"

We sat in moody silence. Caroline shuffled the photographs again.

"I'm going to phone the police," I said at last. "They ought to know about that wine bottle. Why didn't they take it with them? I haven't a clue where it is now though. Somebody will have won it on Leslie's tombola. Anyone in the village could have it. And I'm going to report that Mum is missing."

"I think you're being a bit twitchy about your mum." Caroline glanced at her watch. "Mind you, it's gone eleven now. Actually, I'd better phone my mum and dad too, or they'll be phoning the police about *me*."

I lifted up the receiver, and it beeped to tell me there was an ansaphone message. I pressed one five seven one, then one, to hear the message. I thumbed up to Caroline. It was from Mum.

"Hello Shaun, love. Hope you're not out looking for me. I'm at Cindy's drinking that wine. Must say we're both a bit sleepy. The walk home should wake me up though. See you later — don't wait up." She sounded very cheery.

"She's pissed," I said, grinning with relief. "Her voice is all muzzy."

"Play it again," Caroline said. She listened to it, frowning. "Shaun — what does she mean, *that* wine?"

I felt myself going cold. "I see what you're getting at. That wine. That bottle of strawberry wine. No. Surely not."

"Why doesn't she just say she's drinking wine?"

We listened to the recorded message again. Mum's voice, muzzy and distant; far-away Mum with half a bottle of wine inside her.

"I'll ring her back."

I looked up Cindy's number; it was on a scribbled list of local contacts pinned to the corkboard on the kitchen wall. The phone rang and rang; a bleak, tiny, lonely sound. There was no answer.

"I must have got the number wrong," I said. My voice was shaking. "But I'm sure I didn't." I clicked the phone off, tried again. No answer. "Come on, Mum. Answer me."

But Caroline wasn't listening. She put a hand on my arm. "Shaun," she whispered urgently. "Shush a minute. There's someone outside."

I heard a scrabbling at the door. I rushed to open it and Buster threw herself in, leaping up to slobber over my face in that delightful way of hers, and for once I didn't push her away in disgust.

"At long last, my drunken mother." I ran outside to look for Mum. She was standing by the gate, watching the headlights of a distant car sweeping up into the darkness. She swung her head round to look at me.

"Gosh, am I glad to see you!" she said. "I thought for a minute that was a police car coming down Mam Nick! Heavens, I thought, what's happened now? I hope you didn't phone them to come and find a missing mother!"

I glanced back at Caroline, who'd followed me out and was standing in the doorway. She shook her head slowly, warning me to say nothing. She was right. If Mary Lingworth had phoned the police about us, there was no point involving Mum, not yet. She'd worry her socks off. And if it wasn't the police, she'd still worry her socks off.

"Where've you been?"

"At Cindy's. I left you a message."

"And I phoned you back, and you weren't there."

"Oh, we'd probably set off. Needed to clear our heads! Cindy walked part of the way back with me. Such a gorgeous starry night."

I stood with her for a moment, taking in the silence of the stars, and then the phone rang in the kitchen, startling us all. It was Caroline's father, who had been desperately ringing round all her friends to see if anyone knew where she might be at this time of night. Of course he was in a beautiful mood when he found out she'd been eating chocolate digestives at my house. He told her he would come and pick her up straight away, and she'd better be ready. I glanced at the clock on the cooker. It was past midnight. The evening seemed to have gone on for ever. Mum yawned hugely and sagged into a chair.

"Mum, are you all right?" I asked. "You and Cindy? After that wine?"

"'Course I'm all right! It was very nice wine, I have to say. We didn't mean to finish the bottle, but Cindy insisted on sharing it with me."

"Did she win it in the tombola?"

Mum laughed. "Win it? What are you talking about? We gave it her as a retirement present. Don't you remember? A very nice claret."

"So that strawberry wine is still unaccounted for," Caroline said. "That's worrying."

"Why?" Mum asked, yawning again.

Caroline glanced at me and I nodded. Mum might as well know why I'd been so worried about her. "Because we think it might be poisoned. Like the one that poisoned Miss Lingworth."

"Good heavens, what makes you think that? Win Lingworth wasn't poisoned. She was shot! I thought everyone knew that by now."

"Shot!" My mind was doing slow somersaults, remembering now in vivid detail; colour, sound and smell, that unfamiliar walk with Buster on an overgrown path, sharp blue wood smoke from a cottage chimney, a woman's voice raised in anger — the *crack*! of a gunshot.

"Not poisoned! All that thinking, gone to waste," Caroline moaned.

"You should be glad, for that poor woman's sake," Mum said. "Poisoning must be an agonising death. At least a shooting is quick. Tell you what. It's a fantastic night out there. Why don't you both walk down the lane to meet the car?"

She pushed us gently out of the house, firmly shutting the door so Buster wouldn't follow us.

And that's what we did. The tops of the hills were so white with moonlight that they might have been touched with snow, but the air was warm and soft. Somewhere an owl was hooting. Sheep were calling to each other across the fields. I slipped my hand into Caroline's, and she let it stay, natural.

"How come we didn't know she was shot?" Caroline asked. "All that time we spent, checking up on Gregoria, going to the cottage tonight, for goodness sake, looking for wine-making kit that didn't exist."

"Never mind, you got the photographs. But you've got to take them back."

"In the morning, before school."

"OK. We'll do it together. I'll meet you by the wheelie bins. Half past seven."

"Will you really?"

"'Course I will. We're in this together. Too bad if she's not up. We'll put them on the doorstep. Listen, Caroline. I've got something to tell you. I've been thinking. This is awful, but it might be true. I think I might have heard Win Lingworth being shot."

"*You* did? How?"

"The night it happened, I was walking by the back of her cottage."

Caroline stopped. "You were *where*? You told me you'd never been near the place before the day you found her purse." She pulled her hand away.

"That's what I thought. I'm not hiding anything. I didn't know where I was. Buster took me over some fields after a rabbit or something, and I'd never been that way before. I ended up near a cottage down in a hollow — I could only see the chimney through the trees. And now I realise it might have been hers. And I heard the sound of a gunshot."

"Oh great! You just happen to remember!"

"Well, I did. I know it sounds unlikely, but it's true. I always take Buster on the same walk, but she just dragged me a different way that day. I ought to tell the police what I heard."

"Of course you should."

"But well, if they're going to react like you, maybe it's not such a good idea."

We walked along in silence, tense and uncomfortable with each other now, each of us locked in our own thoughts.

"You believe me, don't you?" I said at last.

"I don't know what to believe," Caroline said slowly. "This has been just about the longest day of my life. I can't think any more, I really can't. But you must tell the police. Do it now."

"The last thing I want to do is to talk to a

policeman tonight."

It wasn't fair, any of it. I wanted the whole awful business to float away. I just wanted to enjoy this time with Caroline, walking together, just the two of us in the moonlight. And now I'd spoilt it. It wasn't my fault that Miss Lingworth had died. It wasn't my fault that she'd been murdered.

We stopped again, and Caroline looked up at me. Her face was silver, her hair a moony black. She looked frail and ghostly, more beautiful than I'd ever seen her.

"We'll decide what to do tomorrow," she said. "We're in this together, remember."

"I think you're —," my throat was tight. I felt as if I was weightless, swimming in the warm silver sea of light. I reached out for her, just her, and our hands touched.

The silver bloomed, dazzling us both, as the headlights of her father's car swung round the bend towards us.

"Tell me tomorrow, Shaun," she whispered.

I jogged back to the house, full of thoughts about Caroline. I expected to be able to go straight to bed, but was surprised to find Mum still up, waiting for me. Her face was drained of colour.

"Is something the matter?" I asked. "Why aren't you in bed, Mum?"

"I've just had a strange phone call. Tell me it isn't true, for goodness sake. A woman called

Mary Lingworth has just rung me."

"She's Miss Lingworth's sister." I tried to sound casual, but my stomach was quaking.

"She rang to tell me that you and Caroline broke into the cottage tonight."

I groaned and slumped into the kitchen chair. Mum sat down opposite me, staring at me as if I'd become some kind of strange creature that she couldn't recognise any more. "Are you completely out of your mind, Shaun?"

"We were looking for clues," I said lamely.

"Clues? Look, this is a serious murder enquiry, not a kids' game. This is going to get you into the worst trouble you can imagine. What the hell were you thinking of?"

I took a deep breath, trying to steady myself. Where to start?

"I'm waiting. You'd better be able to convince me." I've never seen Mum so angry before.

"Is she going to send for the police?"

"No. I am."

"Mum!"

"Convince me, then. I've had enough. I shielded your father when he was getting into trouble. I thought I was doing the right thing, standing by him. But it was not the right thing. He needed to face up to what he had done."

I'd never heard anything about this before. I'd hardly ever heard anything at all about my dad, for that matter.

"What did he do?"

"If you must know, he cheated his employers

109

of a lot of money. I guessed it was happening and promised not to tell anyone if he gave the money back. But he didn't. The company went bankrupt, and it was all his fault. He became violent, threatened his boss, threatened me. He paid for it with his job, and he paid for it with his marriage. He went to prison in the end, and now I don't know where he is and I don't care."

I was devastated. I last saw my dad when I was about five. I couldn't even remember what he looked like. There were no photographs of him in the house, not even a wedding photo. "Why didn't you tell me?"

"I didn't want you to know, that's why. It's not something a child needs to know about his father."

I poured myself a glass of water, drank it in one go. This wasn't real; this was a nightmare. Nightmares can be like thunderstorms, they can go on and on getting louder and more threatening and more frightening till all you want to do is to crawl into the cupboard under the stairs, safe in the stifling darkness.

"This Mary Lingworth," Mum went on. "She said you stole something."

I didn't answer. It sounded pathetic to blame Caroline. We're in this together, we'd told each other.

"What's going on?"

Still nothing. Then — "I don't know, Mum. I can't explain."

"Shaun. If you've got anything at all to do

with this awful business, you've got to tell me, right now."

I couldn't believe what she was saying. I felt as if I was going to start blubbing like a little kid. I pushed my chair round so I was facing away from her, fists clenched tight, so screwed up inside that my guts felt like a tangled mess of knotted string.

"Answer me. Where is it?" she demanded. "Whatever you took, where is it?"

"Caroline's got them. It's just some photographs. We're taking them back in the morning." I swung back to look at her. "Mum, I know it was stupid to go into the cottage. I know it was stupid to take the photographs. But I promise you, I didn't — I didn't..." I couldn't even say it. "Mum you don't really think I did it?"

She shook her head. She was crying, just slow tears trickling down her cheeks, not touched, not wiped away. And then we were both crying.

"I'm glad you told me about my dad. But I'm not like him. I'm not."

"I'll come with you tomorrow," she said, and she stood up and put her arms round me. "We'll sort it out."

14

We waited in Mum's car in a lay-by near the wheelie bins for quite a time, but Caroline didn't turn up. I couldn't believe that she would let me down like this. I messed about uselessly with my mobile, trying to get a signal. There was no way of contacting her. Mum kept looking at her watch.

"She'll come," I promised her. "She said she'd come."

But we were running out of time fast. In thirty minutes the school bus would be passing the end of the lane.

"Perhaps she's already there," I suggested, but I knew that wasn't at all likely. Perhaps she'd told her dad and he'd talked her out of it. I couldn't believe that she wouldn't have come to tell me though.

"Come on," Mum said. "We've waited long enough."

I climbed out of the car, relieved, ready to walk back for the bus, but instead of driving on to work Mum climbed out too and headed for the farm track.

"There's no point going without Caroline," I called.

"There's every point. You've got an apology to make."

So I followed Mum, glancing over my shoulder from time to time, sure that I would hear the sound of Caroline jogging to meet us. I loitered by the gate, but there was still no sign of her, and Mum was banging on the front door. I thrust my fists into my pockets and followed Mum.

There was no answer, so we went round to the back. Mary Lingworth was kneeling on a bit of rug prising weeds out of the flower bed with a little hand trowel. When she saw us coming she looked up, full of smiles.

"I know my sister would want her garden looking after," she said. She stood up, wiping her hands on her skirt. "When that awful ground elder sets in, you never get rid of it unless you grub it out, every bit of it."

"I had that in my garden," Mum nodded. "I got rid of it in the end." She looked round at the little weedy clumps on the path, and the tangled sprawl of the flower beds. "You've got a lot to do. It was a lovely garden, at one time."

"And it will be again. My poor sister let it go, but she wasn't herself, these last few years. Very sad. I'll soon sort it out. I want to fill it with cottage garden flowers again."

She and Mum walked round the garden, totally engrossed in the task of identifying weeds and flowers as if they were judging the Edale horticultural show, and I was left like an overgrown sprig of parsley, abandoned in the corner.

"I've got to go," I said abruptly, and the two women turned round and stared at me, amazed that a herb could speak.

"You came here to say something," Mum reminded me.

"I'm very sorry Miss Lingworth. I shouldn't have broken into your house like that. It was stupid and wrong and I'll never do it again." I'd been rehearsing that since I woke up. I was glad to have it out at last. If I ran, I'd be able to catch the bus.

Miss Lingworth smiled at me and clapped her hands like a child. She's mad, I thought. Completely bonkers.

"And I'm prepared to forgive and forget. After all, we're practically neighbours. We'll put it all behind us now, shall we? Just pop my things on the kitchen table, Shaun." She turned to Mum, chuckling. "He's used to doing that. I believe."

"I haven't got them," I said. I was nearly out of the gate by now in my hurry to get away.

"His girlfriend's bringing them round," Mum told her.

So, it was official. Caroline was my girlfriend. I would never have said it like that, aloud to Mum and the new Miss Lingworth. I grinned happily to myself as I jogged back up the track, jiggling the word in my head as if it was newly minted, sparkling with promise. But where on earth was she, and why had she let me down like this?

She wasn't on the bus. She didn't turn up at school. I tried to ring her at break but my mobile had gone. I couldn't believe it. I wasted time looking for it, tipping the entire contents of my school rucksack on the floor of the corridor. I borrowed a friend's mobile at lunchtime and tried again. No reply. I didn't eat anything, just fretted and sulked and panicked in turn. I daydreamed nightmares. She might have gone to the house before us, just as Mum had suggested. The new Miss Lingworth might have pushed her into the cellar and locked her in there till the police came. No wonder she'd been so friendly to me, so full of smiles and chat with Mum. She didn't need me any more. Oh God, don't hurt her, please don't hurt her, I muttered, and the chemistry teacher raised her eyebrows and flicked a sympathetic smile at me. What did she know? Had there been a phone call to the school? A police hunt for a missing schoolgirl. A lovely daughter, her weeping mother said. Full of life, full of fun. An outstanding pupil, her head-teacher said. My beautiful girlfriend, I told the camera. And I never even told her I loved her.

On the bus home I borrowed another kid's mobile, tried again, no reply. I didn't have her mobile number, it was in the phonebook on mine. I searched through my rucksack again. I *knew* I'd had it that morning. The bus trundled down our lane, past the wheelie bins. I yelled to the driver to let me off there and he refused. "I deliver my precious cargo to their front doors," he said. "That's my job. Don't you know there's a murder hunt on round here? Can't have you kids wandering round on your own."

He wouldn't even let me off when we got to our place, till he'd gone through the tedious business of backing into the next door's farm-yard and turning the bus round. I decided to run straight home and phone her house from ours.

When I burst into the kitchen, the new Miss Lingworth was sitting having tea and chocolate digestives with Mum.

"Where's Caroline?" I shouted.

"Good heavens!" Mum said. "I might ask you where your manners are, Shaun. Sit down and have a cup of tea with us. She'll be here in a minute."

I sank down onto a chair, weak with relief. "How do you know?"

Mary Lingworth pushed the tin of digestives towards me, treating me to one of her cosy smiles.

Mum poured me a mug of tea and handed me my mobile. "You left this in the car this morning. There's a text from Caroline. I read it I'm afraid — the phone rang when I arrived at work and I thought it was mine. I just opened the message automatically."

As casually as I could I clicked on messages. My thumb was twice its usual size, my hand was shaking.

I'll come to yours at 5. C. x

"So I took the liberty of texting her back to remind her to bring the photographs," Mum said.

"OK." My heart was bumping away somewhere in my throat again. 4:55, the cooker clock said. Any minute. Any minute now. I wouldn't relax till I saw her in our house.

"And I invited Mary round to collect her photos and to meet us properly. It's lovely having you here, Mary," Mum said. "Comforting, after that awful week we've had. I know Win's death was a terrible thing, and it's gruesome to think that there's a murderer on the loose, if the police haven't found him yet. But I'm glad the cottage is going to be lived in still, not sold off to a stranger."

If there's one thing Mum loves, it's finding a new friend. She likes to nurture people, especially the shy, lonely ones.

"Your mother's been so kind," the new Miss Lingworth said. "She's given me no end of cuttings from the garden."

"You're more than welcome. Luckily it's just the right time of year for it."

Their voices purred on. I moved over to the window so I could watch out for Caroline, and there she was at last, smiling and waving to me, her hair lifting and falling as she ran up the path, and I breathed again, my blood moved round my veins, the grey world lit up. I beat Buster to the door and let her in.

"You're exactly nine and a half hours late," I told her, my scolding face breaking into a huge grin.

"Soz," she said. Our hands touched briefly, a private kiss.

"Tea?" Mum called. "You don't have milk, do you Caroline?"

Caroline turned back to me and raised her eyebrows when she saw the chummy tea-party round the table. I shrugged.

"Lock the door," she whispered, and when I hesitated, waiting for an explanation, she gave me a 'just do it,' frown. I turned the key quietly, slipped it into my pocket, and followed her.

"You have the photographs?" Mum's new friend licked melted chocolate off her fingers and held out her hand eagerly. Caroline hesitated for a moment then took an envelope out of her pocket and laid it on the table in front of her. Mary snatched it up and peeked in, riffling through the photos, and nodded at Caroline. "Good. Well, that's the end of the matter."

"Family pictures?" I could tell Mum was bursting with curiosity, itching to have a look.

"They're very precious."

Caroline took a deep breath. She looked at me as if she was willing me to give her some support, but I hadn't a clue what was going on. "You might as well know that I've got copies, and I've scanned them onto my computer." She picked the phone from its cradle and keyed in a number. "She's here," she said. "At Shaun Parker's house." She put the phone back on its holder. During all this time none of us moved or spoke. Caroline was like an actor in a play, sure of her lines, and we were an audience who'd gone to the wrong theatre by mistake. "I happen to know that you're not Mary Lingworth at all, and so do the police," she said.

"This is preposterous," the woman said. "What on earth are you talking about?"

"I don't know who you are, but you're not Mary Lingworth. I've been speaking to an Austrian ski-ing coach who has been doing a little research for me." I could hardly believe this was Caroline talking, so serious, so full of confidence, so calm. "As I'm sure you know, Mary Lingworth died last week. A few days, in fact, after her sister."

"I'm not listening to any more of this rubbish." The woman's chair screeched as she stood up. Buster barked at her, startled.

"You can't go," I said. "The door's locked."

Mum had been looking from one to the other of us in total amazement. Now she ran to the door and tried to open it. "So it is! What's happened? What on earth are you two playing at?"

"Mary Lingworth died in a hospital in Austria," Caroline said. "She'd been very ill after a skiing accident that happened two years ago. She never left hospital. Her death has been confirmed by the Austrian police, and Inspector Philip has been told. He's on his way here now."

Mum's face was pale. "Is this true?"

The woman said nothing.

"If you're not Mary Lingworth, who are you?" Mum demanded.

The woman pressed her fingers to her cheeks,

pushing her hands across her face so the skin under her eyes stretched taut and white.

She looked drained and exhausted now, not at all the smiling woman of a few days ago, not even the confident, angry woman of a few minutes ago.

"I know who she is," I said. "She's Win Lingworth's friend. She's on those photographs." I felt bold now too. I moved closer to Caroline, the key to the door clenched in my fist. We were on the brink of solving this mystery, and I didn't just want to hand the woman over to the police and let them ask the questions. "We've even seen your picture on the Internet, at Win Lingworth's award ceremony. We've found out a lot about you. But what we don't know is why you did it. Why did you kill your best friend?"

A puzzled look chased across the woman's face, and then it seemed to clear. She almost looked relieved. At last, I thought, the pretending is over. She bowed her head and opened up her hands, gazing down at her palms as if she held a written confession there.

"My best friend!" she repeated. "Yes, she was. My best friend. I was her only friend, I think. The only person who really understood her. I was her research assistant."

Mum drew in her breath, remembering, as I did, the stilted conversation on the station platform when we met the real Win Lingworth. "She told us about you."

"She would. We were everything to each other.

Win and I worked together ever since we left university. But I didn't kill her."

There was a long pause. No-one spoke, no-one moved.

"She did it herself." She looked at Mum quickly, looking for sympathy.

"Suicide?" Mum gasped. "Oh! The poor woman!"

"I came to visit her — only a couple of weeks ago — and found her dead." The woman's eyes filled up. "It was a dreadful shock. I wanted to surprise her, because it was her birthday. I didn't knock, I came round the back. Late afternoon, kitchen full of yellow light. I thought she was watching the sun setting over Brown Knoll, the way her head was tilted. She didn't move when I came in. There was a gun on the floor."

Mum leaned forward, her hand stretched out, hovering. She wanted to gather this new frail woman in her arms and comfort her, I could see that. The moment passed, the silence imprisoned us, taut as a web, wrapping us inside the horror of the scene.

After a while she began again. "Win was such a brilliant woman, so respected and valued in her field of research and writing. A world authority. One of the best intellects I knew. Her life couldn't end like that, not like that, in such lonely despair. I wanted to protect her from the indignity, the waste. No one must know, I thought, that this great thinker valued herself so little that she took her own life! I just acted without proper thought, without considering the consequences. I was wild with grief and distress. We had been best friends for over forty years. We were closer than sisters."

"So you hid her in the pond," I prompted.

"I had to drag her there. Oh, it was so hard to do! I wrapped her in a little rug she had on the kitchen floor, and dragged her across the grass. Then I rolled her into the pond, yes. The weeds rose up and closed round her as if she had never been. Nobody comes here, I thought. By the time she's found, no one will know what she did to herself. They'll think it was a terrible accident. That she simply fell into her own pond and drowned. How silly, silly of me. I tell you, I was too shocked to think properly. I panicked."

In the silence of the kitchen only the fridge made a sound, a little shivering whirr like an anxious sigh. I was standing by the door again. The key was burning in my palm. Caroline was still by the door that led to the hall. The woman sat between us, her head bowed. She was utterly spent, I could tell.

"What a sad story," Mum said.

"I still don't understand why you pretended to be her, that day I saw you? Why didn't you run away? Why did you lead me to the cottage, with all those things?" I asked.

"It just happened. I'm so sorry." She rubbed her eyes again. "I didn't pretend to be her. It never entered my head that you would think I *was* her. I didn't run away because I had done nothing to be ashamed of. But I couldn't leave her. Can you understand? How could I leave my dearest friend alone like that? No Shaun, you jumped to the conclusion that I was Win when you saw me in the garden, and suddenly I knew that everything would be so much easier if I didn't disillusion you. No explanation needed for her absence. I could even stay on and clear up the place, sort out her academic correspondence, which was my job, after all. I wanted to make it all neat and carefully filed for future researchers in her field. And then — I would just go away. That was my plan."

"But why the trail of lost objects?"

"Ah well, that morning I had woken up with very different thoughts in my head. I tell you, I changed my mind every five minutes! I didn't have a mind — I was just being led by my instincts, and they weren't sound or rational. At that time, I *did* want to leave. I came down the track to the lane to make a phone call — I couldn't get a signal by the cottage. I had actually decided, before I saw you, Shaun, to tell the police that Win's body was in the pond. I didn't want to do it from her landline — didn't want them to think I had been in the house at all, because it would only complicate things if I did. I was going to say that I was just a passing walker who had strayed into the garden and made a terrible discovery. But just when I got my mobile out, testing for a signal, I heard the sound of someone jogging, and without thinking, agitated I suppose, I slipped through a farm gate and hid in a field. Then I realised that I'd dropped my purse. Her purse. I was wearing her jacket. I watched you pick it up and go through it, then I realised that you were intending to bring it back. I panicked. I ran across the field and got ahead of you on the track, and then I thought, what if he does go to the cottage? What if he finds the body? That would be perfect! I wouldn't even be involved. So I left a trail of things just to make sure you came to the right place."

"And waited for me."

"Yes. I wasn't going to of course, but then I changed my mind again. I couldn't leave the place, her place. Not yet."

Mum nodded. She poured another mug of tea and pushed it towards her, but it was ignored.

"And in the end, I did find her," I said slowly. "At least, Buster did."

"Poor Miss Lingworth," Mum murmured.

The woman bowed her head again.

Caroline had been watching and listening all this time, but she'd made no comment. Now she came over to the woman and stood by her.

"You left the cottage eventually. You went away while the police were searching it."

"Of course."

"So why did you go back there last night? Was it just for these?"

She pulled more photographs out of her pocket

and splayed them out.

The woman tried to snatch them from her, but Caroline lifted them out of her reach. "They're the same ones," she said. "I told you. I've scanned them into my computer. And I've sent copies to the police."

She held out the photographs one by one, watching the older woman all the while. From where I was standing I saw her face light up in a full, sad smile. "The dear creature!" she said. "Isn't she lovely! If only I could have saved her."

"If only you had," said Caroline. "What a different story you would be telling now."

"Are you sure she shot herself?" I asked. "It's just that — on the night of her death, I was very near her cottage. And I heard what I thought was a farmer, shooting rabbits somewhere on the hillside."

The woman looked up at me, frowning, absorbing this piece of news. I could hear a car in the lane now. The police had arrived, thanks to Caroline. I unlocked the kitchen door for them, conscious of her watching me. Something's wrong, I thought. Something's weird. Why pretend to be Mary Lingworth? Why the search for photographs in the dark, the visible panic in her face when Caroline told her that she'd made copies of them?

15

The officers that I'd come to know so well stepped out of the car and came into the kitchen. Buster greeted them like old friends.

"Is this the lady?" the gym prince asked Caroline. She nodded. Inspector Philip sat down by the table. Mum indicated the teapot and he lifted his hand in a gesture of refusal.

"The Austrian Police have helped me with some enquiries," he said heavily. "They have confirmed that the lady you claim to be, Mary Lingworth, died in an Austrian hospital three days ago. Have you an explanation for pretending to be her?"

"Not really. Except that I wanted a reason for staying in the cottage for a time. My name is Alison Crow."

Caroline and I looked at each other. Alison Crow. Of course. That was the name on the back of one of the photographs.

"Win Lingworth was my closest friend. She took her own life. I found her, and tried to conceal the body. I wanted it to look like an accident, not suicide."

"Is that the truth?" the Inspector asked her.

"Of course."

"Then perhaps you wouldn't mind coming to the police station with us to make a statement."

She stood up wearily, so weak that Mum leaned forward to help her.

"Poor you," she said. "You've lost your best friend and now there's all this business. Don't be hard on her, Inspector. She did the wrong thing for the right reason."

The woman gave her a grateful smile. "You understand me," she said.

Caroline was leafing through the photographs again. She took two out, and handed them to me. I looked at her, confused, and then at the photographs.

"Why are these so important?" she whispered.

These were the photographs we'd looked at last night. Two little girls, sisters, Win and Mary, arms round each others' waist. Two young women, Win and Alison, proud and happy in their graduation gowns.

And suddenly, I saw what Caroline could see. It was like looking at one of those magic eye pictures made of colored dots, where you stare and stare at them and suddenly you see what didn't even seem to be there before. And when you find it, it's so obvious that you can't believe that no-one else can see it. I looked back at Caroline, and nodded. She was right. The woman was a complete liar. She certainly wasn't Mary Lingworth, because she was dead. Nor was she Alison Crow. I knew exactly who she was.

16

"Inspector, just before you take her, can I ask her something?"

"Go ahead." He was putting his notebook in his pocket, gesturing to the fit one to lead the way out. He wasn't really listening.

"Winifred Lingworth, why did you kill Alison Crow?"

"No, she's not —," Mum began.

The woman seemed to come back to herself. I could see her neck stiffening. She snapped round at me, her eyes blazing.

"I didn't kill her!" she shouted. "She killed me!"

There was no doubt about it. This was the voice I'd heard in the hidden garden, a voice raised in anger before the shot was fired.

"You shot her. I was there," I said. "I heard you say, 'Get out!' I heard you shoot her."

The Inspector shook his head in utter despair and turned his back on me. "What are you suggesting?" he asked Caroline.

"She's not Alison Crow. She can't be." Caroline took the photographs out of my hand and went over to him. "Look at these. Here we have two little girls with their arms round each other. Sisters, Winifred and Mary Lingworth. It says so on the back, look. Not much alike except in their smiles. Do you see? They both have dimples." She showed him the other one. "Here we are. Graduation Day. Winifred and Alison. As alike as sisters, but one has dimples, the other one doesn't. And here," she found another one. "This is an award ceremony a couple of years ago. This woman," she pointed to the figure in the centre, the fixed half smile. "This is supposed to be Winifred Lingworth, receiving the award. But this —" and she pointed to the beaming dark-haired woman at the end of the row. "This *is* Win Lingworth. The lady over there."

We all looked across at the white-haired woman in the kitchen. "Doesn't look anything like her," Inspector Philip said.

Caroline sighed impatiently. "Look at her smile. I knew these photographs were important, but I just couldn't work out why. She smiled at Shaun's mum just now, and I knew. For some reason she and her friend changed places for that award ceremony. She dyed her hair black. She wore glasses instead of the contact lenses she's wearing at the moment. These are easy disguises. Anyone can do that. But you can't disguise dimples! Either you have them or you haven't."

She spread out all the photographs on the table and turned again to the policeman. "I'm not suggesting anything, except that the woman in this kitchen is Winifred Lingworth, the author and acclaimed political analyst. Therefore the woman who was found in the pond was not Winifred Lingworth."

"Who she was then?" the junior Inspector asked, half scornful, half wallowing in admiration.

"She was Miss Lingworth's best friend and research assistant," I said. "Winifred Lingworth spoke very highly of her in an interview she gave in *The Private Lives of Public Figures*." I looked at Caroline. "I finished reading that article last night. I was going to show it to you today — but I didn't realise how significant it was."

Inspector Philip turned the second photograph over, the one of the two smiling graduates in cap and gown. He frowned, short-sightedly making out the words on the back: with Alison Crow.

"You're a very clever girl," said Win Lingworth.

"And she's right?" asked the Inspector.

"Of course she's right, man."

"You are Winifred Lingworth?"

"I've just told you that. Yes, I am Winifred Lingworth."

"So. Let's just go back to what you said before. 'I didn't kill her, she killed me,'" the Inspector quietly repeated the words. He brought a mini recorder out of his pocket and clicked it on. He put it on the table and nodded to his junior to take some notes as well. "Would you care to tell me what you mean by that, Miss Lingworth?"

17

"Alison Crow and I became friends from the first week at university," Miss Lingworth began, simply, dryly. "Very close friends — closer almost than sisters, because we had so much in common. We even looked like sisters, both dark-haired, short-sighted, small! People called us the terrible twins, but we weren't terrible; we were good, bright, academic students. I was cleverer than she was, but she didn't mind. I was cleverer than most people, and it's hard to find friends when you're very bright. People are frightened of you. I'm not saying Alison wasn't bright. She was a brilliant scholar, but she wasn't a genius."

She spoke in a flat matter of fact way, not boasting, just explaining how things were.

"After we graduated I wanted to write political papers and books. Alison suggested that she could be my research assistant. She understood that all I ever wanted was to hide away in my country cottage and think and write. She would do the donkeywork, searching out the journals I needed. She would post them to me, or I would meet up with her and she would pass them on to me."

I remembered again the time we had met her on Edale station; the real Win Lingworth of the dimpled smile, off to meet her research assistant, she had told Mum. The very person that Buster had disturbed in the pond. Dead, and no doubt covered in a white sheet in a police mortuary.

"Go on," the Inspector said. "Alison Crow was your research assistant. You stayed here and wrote."

"Well, eventually my ideas were published and people considered them to be important. I received invitations from universities and governments from all over the world to speak at conferences. I hated the idea! It frightened the life out of me. But she — Alison — persuaded me that it was essential to disseminate my ideas."

"So you swapped names," Caroline said.

Win Lingworth treated her to the smile that had betrayed her identity. "Not exactly, my dear. I kept my name while I was at home. But yes, as far as the world of academia went, we swapped identities. It was so exciting! A wonderful solution! I was Alison, she was Win. She knew my work as well as I did, she had ferreted out all the research material, she had typed everything up for me. And she was an excellent speaker, whereas I would have nearly died of stage fright. So she was wined and dined at all the embassies and foreign offices and government summits — she *was* Winifred Lingworth, the world's greatest modern political thinker! And I hid myself away in my little cottage here among the hills. We were both very, very happy."

The sporty policeman yawned sharply. "So what went wrong?"

"I won an award," said Win Lingworth simply. "It was a very important award. I was very honoured. And I wanted to be there at the ceremony. In disguise, of course. I dyed my hair black, just a colour rinse for the night! Donned the glasses that I had rejected years ago in favour of contact lenses, except when I'm gardening. I even bought myself a posh suit for the occasion. Alison gave a wonderful acceptance speech. I was so proud — proud of her. I had almost begun to believe that it *was* her award, that she *was* Win Lingworth."

"And so had she," I said. "I bet it was Alison who was interviewed for the *Private Lives of Public People* series, not you."

"Of course it was. And she told lies about me. She lied about my sister." Miss Lingworth said bitterly. "It wasn't Mary who turned against me at all. It was Alison who pulled me away from her. She was so jealous of Mary. *She* wanted to be my sister. She wanted to be everything to me. She poisoned my mind against her. And Mary disliked her intensely. Well, when Alison and I started to work so closely together, Mary and I drifted apart."

"And in the end you lost touch with one another. You had no other family, though," Mum put in. "And you were a recluse here; you didn't want anything to do with village life. You had no-one except Alison."

"Exactly."

"And then, you won the award. It was the best thing that had ever happened to you," Caroline said. "And after that, you wanted your life back."

"How well you understand me, child. All of a sudden I wanted to say — this is me! This is my work!"

"But she wouldn't let you."

"She told me no-one would believe me, after all these years. She said she would deny every word of it. I would be a figure of scorn instead of a figure of acclaim. She didn't want to let go of the glory. And I acquiesced, because I couldn't bear the idea of going public, not in that sort of way, dragging the whole story through courts, having my face and my name splashed across newspapers. She would fight me every inch of the way, she said."

She sank back into a chair. I saw how she was twisting her hands in her lap, and how white her knuckles were. Was she telling the truth this time?

"So, you'd lost a friend," Caroline went on. "And then you thought about your sister. You tried to get in touch with her. After all, she was the only person in the world who'd know you as your true self."

"But when you found her, she was seriously ill after that skiing accident." I interrupted. The Inspector raised his wiry eyebrows at me. I don't know whether it was in admiration or contempt. Buster, curled up now in her beanbag bed, whined in her rabbity sleep.

"A terrible accident," Miss Lingworth whispered. "I went to see Mary at once, in Austria. She was in hospital in a pretty town called Graz. I spent over a year with her, nursing her, trying to bring her back to health, feeding her, reading to her. Nothing of the past forty years mattered any more to me. That year in Graz was the best year of my life. I think we made up for all that lost time."

"So why did you come back to England?" the Inspector asked. The sporty one cracked his fingers one after another. It's a really annoying habit. I used to do it on purpose in History.

"Well, I had a wonderful idea. I decided that I would make the cottage comfortable so I could bring Mary home and nurse her here. I missed Edale so much, and I knew she would love it — the peacefulness, the beautiful hills, my lovely garden. I would make her a downstairs bedroom where she could lie in bed and look out on my pond. Mallards come to it, and so does the heron. How she would love it!

"It was all I could think about. I arrived home just before my birthday. I would celebrate it — celebrate finding my sister. I am not a drinker, Inspector, but I knew I had a bottle of strawberry wine in the cellar that I had bought once from a woman in the village."

"Gregoria," I prompted proudly.

"Indeed. So I returned to my little hide-away, full of joy and optimism. I arrived, just as I have described, in the early evening. Sunset time. Oh, how I love this valley at that time of day, with its golden hill slopes and its dark craggy tors against the skyline! I went straight round to my beloved garden. I couldn't believe how it had changed. It was a mess! I know it had been left for over a year — but I grow the sort of flowers that come up year after year with no care and attention. Where were my hollyhocks, my lupins, my Michaelmas daisies, my beautiful rambling roses? They'd all been dug up. Could badgers have done it? In the vegetable patch the pyramids of bean canes had gone, the herbs, everything except a few potato plants going to seed. Everything I loved had been *removed*.

"And then I saw a large black scorched circle where a bonfire had been. I crouched among the charcoal bits and found drawer handles, iron castors, hinges — all the metal bits that wouldn't be burned, and the truth was chiming in my head like a church bell.

"I went to the kitchen, and found the door open. And there she was, sitting in my cottage on a chair that was not mine, at a table that was not mine, in a kitchen that was the wrong colour. There was a jazzy modern hideous rug on the floor stones instead of the rag rug Mary and I had made when we were children. Alison smiled at me and said, 'Welcome to my home, Alison.' I couldn't contain my fury at seeing her sitting in the cottage that I loved so much, as if she owned the place."

'Forget that Alison business,' I said to her. 'It's over. I'm Winifred. I want my name back.'

'Too late,' she laughed. 'You don't expect me to give it up now, do you — after forty years!'

'Get out!' I shouted at her — screamed at her — 'Get out of my home, get out of my life!'

'My home,' she said. 'My life. I live here now.'

"I ran into the little living room, the room that was to be Mary's, ghastly now with lime-green walls, and then up the stairs, into the bedroom, into my writing room — it had all been changed. My mother's old furniture, that had been part of my childhood; the golden rocking chair; the red chaise-longue; the hand-made rugs; the desk that my great-grandfather had made; the water-colour paintings that my long-dead aunt had done; the creaky bed that I had been born in — all gone, burnt, consigned to that funeral pyre in the garden. All replaced by modern plain cheap Ikea stuff.

"I ran back down. 'Get out! Get out!' I screamed. I was pummelling her. I was nearly out of my mind.

'On the contrary, you get out,' she said. Oh! and she was so cold and calm. 'I am Winifred Lingworth, and this is my home. You are tres-passing.'

'*I* am Winifred Lingworth.'

'Prove it.'

"And I knew I couldn't. I felt as if I was losing my mind then.

'Before you leave,' my treacherous friend said,

'I think we should have a drink together, for friendship's sake. I believe it is my birthday.'

"And she produced from the fridge that beautiful glowing rosy bottle of strawberry wine, and two wineglasses, and put them on the table."

"So that's what you meant when you said that she killed you," said the Inspector. "She stole your identity. That is a very serious accusation, and we will of course make a full investigation."

"It won't be in the newspapers, will it?" Miss Lingworth asked. "I couldn't bear it. I really couldn't."

Inspector Philip ignored her. "I will be typing this recording up and taking you to the station and asking you to sign a statement. Now, you don't have to answer this question now, you can ask for a solicitor,"

"I know one," said Mum.

"But I'm asking you, Miss Lingworth. Did you kill Alison Crow?"

She stared at him, trying to drag herself back from the memory of that awful night that she had just described. "Did I kill her? I didn't mean to, if I did." she said at last. "I'm not quite sure what happened, to tell you the truth, and it is the truth, Inspector. She put that wine bottle — my bottle, on the table to celebrate her birthday — my birthday! — and before she could open it I picked up the wineglass and threw it at her with all my strength. It hit her full in the face, smashed on to the table, and broke. She cut her hand on it. Blood flowed quickly onto that disgusting rug of hers. She was wild with fury; I had never seen anyone so angry. She pulled open the kitchen drawer and took out my gun."

The Inspector looked at her sharply. "*Your* gun, did you say?"

"I did. Well not strictly mine, I suppose. The farmer next door lent it to me some time ago — oh, dear, I should have given it back to him, but he never asked for it and I'd forgotten all about it."

"Is that Joe Oldroyd?" I asked.

"Yes indeed, a dear man. He's having such a lot of problems at the moment."

"I know," said Mum. "That wife of his!"

The Inspector cleared his throat. "Why did he give you a gun?"

"Oh, to shoot rabbits, of course! The pesky things wouldn't leave my vegetables alone for five minutes! And I did use it sometimes, just firing into the air, just to frighten them. It seemed to do the trick, but I always kept it handy in case they came back. And so I knew it was probably still loaded. And I was very frightened.

"I ran out into the garden to get away from her. She followed me, waving the gun at me, and I tried to grab it off her then. We were both holding on to it, swaying backwards and forwards on the grass out there. I wanted to get it off her before she did anything stupid. And I wanted her to go, to leave me alone. 'Get out!' I shouted, I do remember that. And then the gun went off, and Alison just — sagged. I stood there. It seemed like hours. I just stood there."

"You didn't kill her," Caroline said.

"But she was dead," I added slowly.

"Exactly." Her voice was a strangled, whispery ghost. "Dead."

18

Buster whined again, her sleep full of night-mares now.

"Then what did you do, Miss Lingworth?" the Inspector asked.

There was a long, hideous silence, broken at last by Caroline. "I know what she did. She covered her up in the kitchen rug, so she couldn't see her. And then she dragged her across the garden to the pond. And rolled her in."

"'And the weeds rose up and covered her, as if she had never been.'" I quoted, as if it was a poem that I'd learnt by heart at school.

"Then she hid the kitchen rug in the cellar," Caroline went on.

"Why?" the Inspector asked Miss Lingworth.

"There was blood on it, from the broken glass. She couldn't wash it off." Caroline said.

"Perhaps you would let Miss Lingworth tell her story," the Inspector said, "But I'm intrigued to know how you know so much."

Caroline tapped the brainy side of her head. "There's a pale patch on the kitchen floor where a rug used to be, for a start. And I found a tiny splinter of glass under the kitchen table. But down in the cellar I could still smell damp carpet. Couldn't you?"

I remembered the sharp, fusty smell down there. "And blood."

The Inspector nodded. "You are correct. The rug is now in police possession, of course."

I couldn't help feeling proud of Caroline. But there were still bits of the story that didn't quite fit. A woman goes through all that, and the next day she's digging up potatoes in the garden and *smiling*! I turned back to Win Lingworth.

"You didn't seem very upset that day I saw you."

"Upset? Why should I be upset? I was free! I had my *self* back, in the only place where I had ever been myself — my own home."

I suppose I could understand that, just about, if I didn't think too hard about the murky depths of her pond. "But then you tried to put the blame on me!"

Miss Lingworth made a fluttering, helpless gesture with her hands. "It was just as I told you. I panicked. I wanted someone to find the body and report it to the police. As it happens, you weren't the only person to come to my cottage that week."

"Joe Eldridge visited you." The younger policeman said, quickly, obviously trying to get it in before Caroline did.

"The farmer. He was very upset. He had a problem, and he had heard that I was a clever woman and might be able to help him. I told him, my business is world politics, not family law."

142

"What did he come about?" the Inspector asked.

"I'm not prepared to discuss it. He came to me in confidence."

"And that's how he found Molly's binoculars on the gate," I said. Well, some things were beginning to make sense, after all. But still not everything. "And then you ran for it. I saw you in Sheffield — and you saw me, though you pretended you hadn't."

Miss Lingworth shook her head. "Did you see me? I don't remember seeing you. I was in a daze. I had had very bad news from the hospital in Graz. My dear sister had died."

My mother had been listening carefully to all this. At this point she seemed to make her mind up. She moved forward and took both Miss Lingworth's hands in hers.

"How terrible for you. I'm so glad you'd had a chance to make it up with her."

Poor Mum was completely overcome then. Mum's like that. But Miss Lingworth was still holding herself together. She talked quietly and thoughtfully, as if she was trying to remember a dream she had had, and describe it before it all floated away.

"I've just come back from her funeral. I flew home yesterday."

"Right," said the Inspector. Absent-mindedly he helped himself to a chocolate digestive. The other one leaned forward and did the same. They munched comfortably in the thinking silence.

"Things are beginning to make sense to me. Your sister had just died, you say. So why did you come here pretending to be her?"

Caroline opened her mouth to speak, and the Inspector gave her a warning look under his shelf of bristling eyebrows.

"Let Miss Lingworth tell her story."

"It all seemed so easy," Miss Lingworth said. "I could begin again, if I was Mary. Everyone thought I was dead, so how could I live in my cottage? It was the only thing I wanted to do. It would be so much easier to move back in as Mary. No fuss. No more writing. All that was behind me. I would be a simple, retired woman living in her sister's house, growing vegetables and flowers. Everybody would leave me alone."

"But you needed to destroy the family photographs," Caroline butted in at last. "Mary was tall and thin, blond curly hair; lively, energetic, the sporty type. Not a bit like you. You wanted to destroy all these photographs. Especially this one."

She put one of the photographs into Miss Lingworth's hands.

"No, you're wrong this time," Win Lingworth said. She smiled at last. "This is the one I wanted to keep, to remind of my sister. To remind me of how much we loved each other in those days, before that evil woman Alison Crow came on the scene. Two little girls, smiling out of the past of over fifty years ago. I never want to part with this one. Never."

144

19

The two policemen led Win Lingworth out to the police car. We followed them. I think Mum would have gone to the police station with her if they'd allowed her to. Miss Lingworth got into the car without a word, just a quick, quiet white-faced glance at me, and I thought about the morning when her garden had been full of sunshine and she had presented me with the bottle of wine. How happy she had been then. If only it was true that she had been trying to write a murder mystery, rather than being the major player in one.

The police car drove away slowly, and Mum and I stood and watched as the lights dipped and bobbed along the bumpy lane, swung up and up the steep pass of Mam Nick, and out of sight.

"What a story," Mum said sadly. "What a tragic story. You were very clever to work it all out."

"We were completely wrong at first," Caroline said. "We were convinced it was something to do with that bottle of wine."

"Ah, that wine!" Mum smiled. "I shouldn't really tell you this, but there's a funny story about that strawberry wine, if anything about this terrible affair can be funny. I gave it to the vicar for the bottle tombola, as you know, but the poor man couldn't resist it — and he decided to drink it himself! It did look very tempting. Anyway, he said it had been kept too long and had gone really sour. It tasted awful! So he had to pour the whole lot away! Cindy said she'd bought one from the same batch last summer, and it was disgusting. She said poor Gregoria was very embarrassed about it. Oh, I've had a really gossipy afternoon with Cindy! Did you know Rhoda has gone back home to Joe Eldridge? She didn't take to farming at all, though she liked the idea of owning one, so she'd upped and gone home to Grandma. But Molly wasn't having any of it and she's packed her back to him. 'It's your home, it's where you belong,' she told her. And she's right. Home is so important. Well, look how important it was to Win! So, anyway, poor Joe's been acting like a crocodile with toothache while she was away, and nobody could blame him. Out on his tractor every night, just crawling up and down the fields. That's probably why he went round to see Win, to ask her advice. I was thinking of recommending my solicitor friend to him."

"Well, that's all the mysteries solved then," I said. "Oh, except Jenny. The postie. How come she saw me going to Miss Lingworth's cottage, when I didn't see her?"

"Did you ever see a woman on a mountain bike round there?"

Aha! Mystery solved.

I walked Caroline back to her place, my arm over her shoulder, her arm round my waist, her head resting just lightly against me. We said nothing, nothing at all, just enjoyed that amazing togertherness, till we came to Win Lingworth's track. We stopped by the wheelie bins.

"It's just that part of the evening that Win described, sun turning the hills golden, birds roosting in the trees; Edale at its most peaceful." Caroline said. "Perfect."

"Perfect. Just us." I put both my arms round her, my face in her hair. I was dizzy and warm and weak and strong for her.

"What will happen to her?"

"I don't know. It's a weird story isn't it? But I don't really think she did anything wrong." I stroked her hair. "It wasn't a case of murder. after all."

"They might give her a short sentence, I suppose." She frowned, looked up at me. In the low sunlight her eyes were bluer than ever. "If she does go to prison, should we try to keep her garden going for her, till she gets out? Like, put in a few plants, keep it weeded?"

"Anything," I said. "Anything at all. As long as we do it together."

I bent forward, and at last, at long last, we kissed.